# Copper

By Ceri Bladen

## Prologue
*September*

In the darkness of her bedroom, Victoria ripped herself out of her troubled dream.  She sat up, wiped the sweat from her brow and checked to see if she'd woken her sister.  Satisfied that Anne was still asleep, Ria took a calming breath then placed a hand over her fluttering heart.

Now fully awake, Ria was glad that her dreams had disappeared, but, as reality seeped through, so did her fear and guilt.  "Oh no, what have I done?" she whispered.

## Chapter 1
*Eight months earlier*

In the dimly lit, cold bedroom, Ria sat at the aged, brown-spotted mirror and looked at her reflection. Grabbing a handful of her curly, copper-coloured hair, she attempted to get it under control. She hated putting it up. It was much easier to let it curl naturally over her shoulders. But, work needed it tied back so that it didn't get stuck in the machinery.

Finally secured, Ria reached for her mascara. Grabbing the small brush, she rubbed it against the black block and stroked it along her naturally long upper eyelashes. When she finished her eyes, she rubbed petroleum jelly along her lips, for shine. She inspected her reflection, happy with the subtle results.

Ria would have loved to own newer makeup. Some of her friends had the new type wand mascara, but she didn't have spare money to spend on luxuries. The reality of it was that she made do with family hand-me-downs.

In the corner of the mirror, Ria caught sight of her younger sister snuggled in bed. Anne would be warm under the sheets and woollen blankets, even though the bedroom was cold. Since she was younger, she'd shared a room with her sister. Now Ria was older, there were times she longed for privacy, but she was realistic enough to know her family could not afford a bigger house on her Dad's mining wage package. Instead, whenever she was in need of solitude from her large family, Ria took herself off down to the seaside. It was during those quiet times that Ria appreciated living in a city where you could be in amongst the houses one minute, and the next, by the sea.

Knowing it was getting late, she stopped daydreaming, needing to get to work. As she moved, the scrape of the chair disturbed Anne.

"Is it time to get up?"

Ria cringed, she hadn't intended to wake her. "Sssh, go back to sleep. You have another half an hour before it's time to get ready for school."

Anne's only response was to pull her pillow over her head.

Ria smiled at her sister's lack of response. She would love to snuggle back down, too. Anne moaned about this time of year, but Ria didn't mind it. It was the time when everyone, including nature, prepared for the Winter. Her mother was already busy with jams, and pickling the fruit and vegetables that her Dad brought from his allotment. Once bottled, they were stored in neat rows on a cold slab in the larder, to keep them cool. But, it had been difficult this morning, getting out of the warm bed into the cold bedroom. Their fire had long since died, and as no one would be using the room until the evening, the fireplace remained cold.  While they were at work or school, her mother would clear them out and restack the fireplaces for when they returned.  Some 'well-off' neighbours used radiators, but money was tight in the Dillwyn household. Central heating was not a priority.  Besides, her father and brother worked down the coal mines and over the years, Ria had listened to far too many discussions about the effects on mining communities if people stopped using coal!

When she noticed her breath cloud in the frigid air, Ria swapped her thinner cardigan for a thicker woollen. Her neighbour, Marge, had knitted it for her last Christmas.  As Ria buttoned her cardigan, her mother's voice interrupted her thoughts.

"Are you lot up yet?  Your breakfast is on the table.  You'll all be late for work if you don't get a move on!"

Not bothering to reply, Ria grabbed her bag and crept across the bedroom. She quietly closed the door giving Anne her precious extra minutes in bed.

While Ria made her way down the landing, she noticed the carpet looked even more threadbare than usual. She bent down for a closer inspection of the fraying hole. It upset her that even though her Dad had a dangerous job as a miner and worked hard, they still lived 'hand to mouth'. It wasn't as if her Dad was one of those men that spent his pay packet down the pub, before giving the remains to her their wives. Ria sighed and straightened back up wishing her pay package would stretch some more.

When she passed her brothers' bedroom, Ria peered through the doorway, and around at the mess. Clothes were strewn everywhere, beds unmade, and, like hers, the fireplace cold with ash. Amidst all the carnage was Tom, one of her brothers. He hadn't noticed her yet as his hands fumbled around a drawer. Ria watched him scowl until he found a matching pair of socks. She shook her head in amusement. "What a mess, Tom Dillwyn."

Tom looked up, a smile warmed his previously scowling face.

"Morning, sis."

"I feel sorry for any girl you end up with. She will have to spend all her time cleaning up after you."

"Yep." Tom sat down on his unmade bed to put on his socks. A smile continued to play on his lips. "But, why would I want to end up with *one* girl when there are so many?"

"Tom."

He laughed at the haughty look that appeared on Ria's face.

She scowled at him. This was the part of her brother that irritated her. He was too used to women falling for him.  Since he hit adolescence, he *always* had a girlfriend - usually a different one every week. Ria understood that they fell for him, he was handsome, but it didn't sit well with her that he went through so many. His reputation made her know that looks weren't always a good thing, they had too many women to choose from.  As much as she loved her brother, Ria knew that when she found someone, she wanted to be the *only* one. Subconsciously she stayed away from anyone remotely like her brother, they were liable to break her heart.

Ria straightened up from the door jamb and wagged a finger at him.  "I heard you trying to sneak in late. From the Red Lion, no doubt.  Trying not to wake up Mam and Dad?"

"What me, your responsible older brother?"

Ria couldn't stay annoyed at him for long, She laughed and watched him pull his six-foot frame off the bed.  It amazed her that he was so tall when she was only a couple of inches over five feet' like her mother.

As he passed, Tom gave her nose a playful twist and nudged her towards the stairs.  "Bet Mam could use the porridge for wallpaper paste by now!"

Ria and Tom laughed as they burst through the kitchen door. Immediately, the heat of the cooker and the smell of porridge and coffee hit them.

"Good morning," said Ria.

"Morning," replied both her parents.

Ria walked over to the coffee pot and poured two cups. Carrying them, she walked over to the pan of milk on the stove her mother had warmed earlier. After she had finished, she handed one to Tom. Ria wrapped her hands around her cup and sighed in contentment. She took a sip. Her parents preferred a traditional cup of tea, but after being introduced to fresh coffee by her friend, Ria favoured coffee to wake her up.

Evan looked up from his porridge. It warmed his heart to see his wife and children in the morning before he started his shift down the coal mine. It was a place he couldn't honestly say he would come home from. He glanced at the kitchen clock and realised they were running late. "Come. Sit and eat your porridge. Your Mam didn't get up early to make it only for it to go cold."

"Okay, Dad." Ria knew her father well enough to know it was a light-hearted reprimand. She walked around Michael, who had already polished off his breakfast, towards her father's chair and gave him a huge, noisy kiss on the cheek. "Sorry, Dad and Mam for being late this morning." She winked at her young brother, Sam, who smirked into his cereal bowl. She laughed when her father grunted.

Ria picked up a bowl and helped herself, adding a generous helping of homemade raspberry jam. She glanced towards her mother intending to thank her for the jam, but she noticed a tired look on her face. "Are you all right, Mam?"

"Yes, love. Just tired."

"Aw, how is Johnny this morning? I heard him coughing during the night."

Johnny was Ria's youngest brother. He was ill. He'd caught measles when he was a baby, and after that, one infection after another. It wore her parents out mentally and financially. Johnny was the reason Ria had gone to work in the clothes factory straight after school, instead of following her dreams of becoming a nurse. The extra wages she brought in helped towards medicines for Johnny and made it slightly easier for her parents.

"No, he didn't have a good night, but he's resting at the moment."

"Good," said Ria.

"On your way to work, would you mind getting Dr Bevan to call in today, Victoria?" Megan wiped her wet hands on her apron.

"Yes, of course, Mam." Ria smiled at her mother but felt down. She knew Dr Bevan had been visiting Johnny more and more over the last six months. She tried to squash her unease. She didn't want her feelings to show, her parents didn't need to worry about her as well.

"Evan, you will have to leave me money today. I need to pay our bills at the Post Office. I couldn't the last time I was there because I didn't have enough. So I'll sort it out today. Doris will keep an eye on Johnny for me."

Doris was a dear neighbour. Company and help for Megan while everyone was out for the day. Doris lost her husband in a mining accident seven years before. They'd never had children, she was on her own, so the Dillwyn family had welcomed her in as one of their own.

"I'll get my wallet."

"No need, Dad." Tom reached into his back pocket and drew out his wallet. "I've got some spare money. I won a little last night, and I want you to have it."

Ria watched as Tom gave his mother the money, along with a kiss and a hug. She smiled as she knew what was going to come next.

Megan wiped her hands on her apron and forced a scowl on her face. She was going to berate Tom for gambling down the Red Lion, but she also appreciated the money. "You've been down that Red Lion again playing cards with all those scoundrels. I've told you..."

While her mother told Tom off, Ria watched her father place his bowl in the sink and walk over to Megan.

Evan wrapped his arms around his wife's waist, and kissed her hair. "Leave the boy be, Meg. He's only twenty. Leave him have some fun. Responsibilities will come soon enough."

Megan turned slightly and eyed her husband. "Aye, you're right."

"As normal," Evan said, knowing it wasn't true.

"Humpf. Come on the lot of you, off to work. Leave me in peace to get this house sorted." Megan waved her arms, complete with a tea towel, to exaggerate her point.

"Going," said Sam.

"Me, too," replied Michael.

"Don't forget to grab your lunches," said Megan to all of them.

Ria placed her mug in the sink and went to kiss her mother. She walked over to the coats. As she put her coat on over her work clothes, Ria noticed that the grey wool had started to look threadbare. She sighed, slightly downhearted, loving to purchase a new one, who wouldn't? But her spare money needed to go towards food and Johnny, not her vanity. "Mam, do you think Doris could do some magic on my coat when I come home from work?"

"Of course. I'll ask her today."

"Thanks."

Megan inspected the damage and wished they could afford to buy Ria a new one.

"I've got one you can borrow while she is repairing it," said Megan.

"Great. Thanks, Mam."

Megan turned to give Evan a goodbye kiss.

Ria smiled at her parents' affection towards one another. There'd been a time, when she was little, that she was embarrassed when they kissed or cuddled. But not now. It was what she wanted when she married. Not that Ria wanted that yet, she was only eighteen.

Now she was an adult, she ventured into the city with her friends, Karen and Sally. They regularly went to the Odeon cinema to watch a new film. A couple of evenings, Ria had gone out with John, Dr Bevan's son. For Ria, there was nothing romantic about it, though her friends kept telling her he was a 'good catch'. But Ria wasn't interested. He didn't stir any romantic ideas in her, she just enjoyed his friendship because he made her laugh.

In fact, Ria was a true romantic at heart, even though reality tried to rob her of her dreams, now she was older. From a young age, she dreamed about being swept off her feet by her soul mate. Karen and Sally thought she was mad, but she still held on to her fantasy. Karen told her that she would never settle down if she were only looking for 'the one'. Karen then went on to say that she'd kissed many frogs looking for her prince! Whatever her friends thought, Ria wasn't going to settle for less.

The cold, autumn air hit her exposed skin when she pulled open the front door. She didn't mind, she was going to be in a stuffy factory for most of the day.  She waited for her father and brother to exit and closed the door.

As they walked to work, Ria listened to the morning birds. A smile touched her lips when her dad pointed to a robin on the neighbour's garden wall. Winter was obviously on its way.

Ria stopped when they reached the end of the road.  "Dad, I'm going this way today."

"Why?" asked Michael.

"Because I'm going to fetch Dr Bevan."

"Okay, love," said Evan.

Ria gave her father a tight hug. "Be careful down the mines today. It poured down last night, and you know how the mines flood."  A concerned crease marred her forehead.

Evan gently tapped his daughter's nose. "It's what we do and what your grandfathers did before us. Be proud," Evan quoted the sentence he always used after she voiced her concerns.

"You look after yourself, and you, Michael." Ria poked her brother in the chest with her finger.  "Love you both, see you for dinner tonight." She waved to them and watched them walk away. An easy banter already between them.

Ria quickened her pace. She hurried up the narrow alleyway to Dr Bevan's house because she didn't want to be late. Work was strict with clocking in times. She rushed past one backyard after another, and she cringed, hoping that the barking dogs didn't wake the whole neighbourhood up.

Reaching Dr Bevan's, she raised her hand to grab the brass lion knocker on the door. Ria liked it but had always found it a little grand for the house. She quickly knocked and took a step back. Ria hoped she wasn't disturbing the Doctor at too early an hour. Within seconds, she heard footsteps approach the door.

"Well, good morning, Victoria. What can I do for you?" Mrs Bevan, a short, stout woman, similar to her husband, greeted Ria with a friendly smile.

"Is Dr Bevan able to go and look in on Johnny today? He had a bad night, and Mam is worried."

"No problem love, I'll ask him to add him onto his rounds today. But I'll have to warn you, I don't know how fast he'll be there, with measles breaking out all over town, he is busy."

"Mam will be in most of the day, or Marge, so that isn't a problem," she replied. The smile on Ria's face smile quickly turned into a wince when she saw Mrs Bevan turn around and shout upstairs.

"John, love, hurry! Ria is here. Come and say hello."

Ria had enjoyed her evenings with John, courtesy of Mrs Bevan's matchmaking, but that didn't mean that she appreciated Mrs Bevan's attempts to throw them together this early in the morning. She sighed with frustration but then felt guilty.

She loved John's easy-going company, but that was all. Their time together had been good, until recently when John had made his interest in her clear. It made her uncomfortable. Not wanting to string him along, she'd stopped arranging to see him. But, after a chat with Karen and Sally, she was persuaded to give him another chance. Unsure what to do for the best, she did. She liked him and didn't mind the odd kiss, but she certainly didn't want to take things any further. But so far, John seemed to be getting mixed messages.

John flew down the stairs at breakneck speed. "Morning, babe. And what do we owe this pleasure?" He grinned. "Missing me?"

"Oh, he's a one." Mrs Bevan glowed while giving her only child a beaming smile. "Ria has asked your Dad to go and check in on Johnny. Perhaps you could ask Ria to go out tonight to cheer her up?"

John eyed his mum dryly before an amused smile lit up his face. "Thanks, mam, but I can arrange my life. Myself. Have you got my lunch ready? Then I can walk to work with Ria."

"Of course. I'll get it now."

Ria exhaled. She tried to feel thrilled at the thought that he wanted to spend time with her. John was handsome with blue eyes, wavy blond hair, and strong jawline. Even his slightly misshapen nose, which her brother had broken in a game of rugby, didn't deter from his looks. But regardless, Ria never experienced butterflies or mind numbing feelings when she saw him. She wanted to.

"Thanks, Mam. You're a good one."

Mrs Bevan turned and walked down her hallway.

When she was out of ear-shot, Ria said, "I'm already late John, I will see you another time." She started to turn away.

John grabbed her arm. He turned towards his mother's direction. "Don't worry. I will pick something to eat on the way, I don't need the sandwiches," he shouted down the empty hallway. He took his coat off the rail and closed the door. "So, about tonight? Do you fancy doing something?"

"Ah, I don't know John. I need to get home to help Mam with Johnny."

John's face fell.

"He isn't sleeping at night time. And Mam isn't resting because she is busy with the housework."

"No problem then. You need to help her."

"I should be at home all the time to help, but we need the money that I bring in. Anne takes time off school to help, but the headmaster had a word with my parents about her missing too much school." Tears threatened to flow, so she took a steadying breath. "Hey, look at me being all sensitive this morning."

John stepped nearer and gathered her in his arms. He kissed the top of her curly red hair. "You can be sensitive on me anytime, babe, anytime."

Ria relaxed into the hug. She did enjoy the comfort his arms gave her. Worrying about Johnny's illness and money was a lot to bear at such a tender age. Sometimes overwhelming her. These times she valued John's company because he was dependable and kind. But, then she felt guilty for using him for comfort and not wanting more from him.

"Well." He moved his hands onto her shoulders. He took a step back. "If you don't fancy meeting tonight, let me, at least, walk you to and home from work."

"Thanks, John, thanks for being understanding."

They walked the rest of the way with his arm draped around her shoulders. Coming from a large family, this was the type of contact Ria was entirely comfortable with.

## Chapter 2

The first thing to assault Ria as she walked into the factory was the noise. It was a welcoming, familiar sound - gossiping workers and the racket of machinery warming up. Ria made her way towards the lockers, the place where everyone congregated for their morning natter.

In between the gossip, coats were hung up in exchange for overalls and hats.

Ria put her work cap over her braided hair and donned her overall.

Sally, Ria's friend since Infant school, sidled up to her.

Ria eyed her friend. Sally was tiny, even smaller than her. She reminded Ria of a beautiful fairy pixie she'd read about in school. She could imagine the blonde haired, sea-blue eyed Sally sitting on top of a mushroom singing to enchant passing humans. Sally was oblivious to her charms, shy with anyone she didn't know.

"Was that John I saw you with this morning?" Sally said.

With all the background noise, Ria didn't notice Sally's sigh. "Yes, I had to go and ask his father to pop in on Johnny."

"Is Johnny all right?" Sally asked, concern lacing her voice.

"He's the usual. Mam is tired, though."

"Poor Megan."

"John was there, and he walked me to work."

___ "That's romantic."

"Romantic? We only walked to work."

"I wish I had someone to walk me to work in the morning, I have to endure my immature brother."

Ria laughed. "I've told you. There's nothing romantic going on between John and myself. I enjoy his company, but nothing else. In fact, he is like a brother to me. I know that Karen keeps telling me to carry on seeing him, but it is taking a while for me to fall for him."

Ria closed her locker, failing to detect the lowering of Sally's shoulders.

Despite being good friends with Ria, Sally had omitted to tell her that she was secretly in love with John. She had been for a good number of years. During the final year of school, Sally had finally plucked up the courage to tell her friends. But, just as she was about to let them in on her secret, John sauntered over. She only had to witness the look in John's eyes as he looked at Ria, to know she didn't stand a chance with him. There was no competing with that look of longing. Sally took a step back and hid her feelings. Teasing Ria about him took some of the hurt away. "Pass him over to me when you have finished with him, then."

Ria's eyebrows rose and then laughed.

Sally giggled to hide her hurt feelings. She worried her bottom lip hoping that Ria hadn't picked up on her feelings for John. Sometimes she found it difficult to hide her emotions.

They both turned when their boss, Mr Jones, passed them. He was deep in conversation with a man they hadn't seen before.

Ria watched the strange who dwarfed her rotund boss. She felt an odd pull in her stomach. He was the most attractive man she had ever seen. He had jet black hair, and taut, tanned skin stretched over prominent cheekbones and a strong, square jaw. His broad shoulders tapered down to long legs, with, Ria noted with a grin, a very decent bottom. Well dressed in grey slacks, a white shirt, and dark grey jacket, he was obviously a man with money.

Ria glanced down at her overalls. She was glad it covered her bland clothing, which had seen better days. Her head snapped back up as she watched him make his way to Mr Jones's office. It had been a long time since anyone new had ventured into the factory, or even into the village. Especially someone who looked like him!

The stranger seemed so engrossed in his conversation that he surprised Ria by looking straight at her when he closed the door to the office.

She was embarrassed getting caught, but couldn't pull her gaze away. Realising she was finding it difficult to swallow, she prayed she wasn't blushing – a curse of her porcelain skin colour. Even though he'd only looked at her for mere seconds, she was shaken. It felt as though he had seen straight into her soul. Feeling vulnerable, a shiver made its way through her body. "Sally, who's that with Mr Jones?" she whispered.

Sally shrugged her shoulders. "I've got no idea. Handsome, though."

"Yes," Ria muttered, still feeling shell-shocked.

Overhearing their conversation, Marge, the factory gossip, made her way over to them. "He must have something to do with the Templetons. They own this plant."

Sally rolled her eyes.

Undeterred, Marge continued. "You can tell by the dark brooding looks. Like Heathcliff, isn't he?" She chuckled and crossed her arms over her ample bosoms. Marge, a loud lady, had worked at the factory since the age of sixteen. Being a veteran, she always knew the gossip, which she liked to impart regularly. "He must be a Templeton. I can tell." She nodded, before turning to include others in her conversation. "Mind you, if he is, he won't get too close to us *mere* workers. Oh no. Well perhaps, but only for slap and tickle." She tapped her foot on the floor and tempered her voice to impart the rest of her gossip. "A couple of years ago, the youngest Templeton boy, came into work."

"Darren," one of the workers supplied the name.

"Ay, that's right. Darren. To *'learn the ropes'* they said. Did some learning all right – with the ladies!" She tutted. "Poor Sarah Davies. She thought he was going to propose to her after he had..." Marge looked around the group making sure she had all their attention. "Well, you know what! Well, her family found out and weren't too pleased. They moved away from the area. The gossip was too much for them in the end."

Ria silently wondered how much of that gossip was spread by Marge and her kind.

"Do you know what Darren supposedly said after she had left? That his family would never allow him to marry a worker from the factory! She was just a bit of fun! Broke poor Sarah's heart and her family, too. Yes, mark my words, if any of those Templeton boys show interest in you – it isn't long term!"

Morgan Templeton had not had a good start to the week.

His father phoned him late Friday night to say he'd gone over the Swansea factory's accounts, and he'd noticed discrepancies. David, his father, had requested – no, demanded - that Morgan left London *immediately* to come to Swansea to find out what was happening, and who couldn't be trusted to work for the Templetons.

Morgan found it difficult to be calm and patient with his father's request.  He knew it didn't matter to his father that he had a date planned for Saturday or that he'd spent years learning to be an accountant so that he could move away from his loving, but sometimes constrictive family. But, there was no use arguing. When his father demanded, his father usually got.

Morgan enjoyed living on his own in his London apartment because for the first time in his life, he felt free. Free from all the demands his family put on him when he was around. He knew they loved him, but felt stifled when he was near them. Even though he loved his hometown of Swansea, for his sanity he needed his life.  His bachelor life, with a never ending supply of available women for dates. He was only twenty-seven and knew there was plenty of time to continue enjoying the wonderful company of women before he had to settle down to responsibilities.  Until his Dad phoned.

Morgan pushed his thoughts to the back of his mind and concentrated on his discussion with Mr Jones. He followed him across the factory floor and up the creaky metal stairs to the room that was going to be his office for the next couple of weeks. Or at least, until Morgan could discover what was happening to the money. Something he wanted it to be dealt with as soon as possible so that he could go back to his normal life.

When listening to the ramblings of Mr Andrew Jones, the factory supervisor, it became apparent that he was unaware that personnel staff were being observed. Thinking on his feet, cursing his father for not giving him the whole story, Morgan made up the simple ruse that he was here to learn all the ins-and-outs of the family business.

When they reached the office, suspended above the factory floor, Morgan turned to close the door. For some unknown reason, he felt drawn towards something. He looked for the source. He locked onto the gaze of one of the workers. For a mere moment, everything stopped. Morgan did not hear or see anything else until the girl lowered her eyes, and colour shaded her cheeks. With a puzzled smile and a shake of his head, Morgan closed the door on the factory below.

Morgan scanned the room that was to be his office while Mr Jones pointed out a couple of things. He had been in here many times with his father, but he let Mr Jones carry on.

As a child, one item that always fascinated him was the large one-way mirror that dominated one length of the room. From it, an overall view of the factory was possible. His father had it installed so he could 'keep an eye' on everything, without having to go downstairs.

"This is your desk." Mr Jones needlessly pointed out the only desk in the room. It was an old, large, walnut desk, behind which was a comfortable green leather seat.

"Thanks." Morgan smiled. He remembered the times his father allowed him to swivel around on the chair.

"I'll be over here."

Morgan turned and noticed a simple put up table opposite. Obviously, for Mr Jones while Morgan was there.

In one corner of the room was a settee. He'd spent many hours sitting on it with his mother, waiting for his father to finish work.

The table next to it had a coffee pot, teapot, and milk laid out on it.

"Would you like tea or coffee, Mr Templeton?" Mr Jones asked.

"Coffee, please. Black. But please, call me Morgan. I keep thinking my father is here."

Andrew Jones laughed as he poured. "Okay, Morgan. In that case, call me Andrew. But I would suggest the workers still refer to you as Mr Templeton?"

"Whatever you suggest."

Andrew handed him his coffee.

"Right to business then." Morgan pointed to the stack of files on the desk. "Mr Jones, sorry… Andrew, would you like to explain these to me?"

After a couple of hours, Morgan finished the majority of the paperwork.

Weary, he rubbed his hand over his stiff neck. The green leather of the chair creaked when Morgan stood up to elevate his discomfort. He looked over at Mr Jones, who seemed engrossed in another pile of paperwork. He rolled his shoulders and heard a bell ring.

It was for the workers tea break.

The noise reminded him of the fresh coffee that had been brought in not three minutes earlier. Morgan walked over and poured himself one.

"Coffee, Andrew?"

"Tea for me, please."

As he poured himself the drinks, Morgan found himself wondering if the woman he had spotted this morning would be enjoying her break with the others.  The thought made him smile to himself.

Receiving a preoccupied smile from Andrew in thanks for the tea, Morgan walked up to the window.

Morgan spotted her quickly, talking with a group of workers. He noticed a quickening of his pulse. It didn't bother him. It was something he felt comfortable with because he enjoyed appreciating women.  But, what did bemuse him was the fact that he couldn't stop watching her.  He took pleasure in watching her throw her head back and laugh, watching dimples appear on her cheeks, watching her touch her friend's arm in conversation.  Morgan had an urge to know more about her. He half turned to question Andrew, while he tapped the window with his finger.  "Who is that woman with the red hair?"

"Mmm, what? Oh!  Sorry, just finishing off here. The girl with the red hair?  Well... that must be Victoria Dillwyn.  Her family and friends call her Ria."

Morgan continued to watch her.

"Nice family.  Father and brother work down the mines if my memory serves me correctly.  The younger brother isn't well at the moment, which is why Ria comes to work. To pay the bills and all that. Think she has one sister and three brothers, or has she got four...?"

Once Morgan found out what he wanted, he barely listened to the rest of Andrew's ramblings. He made a mental note to remember, in future, once you got Andrew Jones talking, he was hard to stop.

When Morgan continued to look at her, a pleasant sensation moved through his system.

The bell for the workers to go back to work made him jump.

Looking down at his cup, he realised he'd spent the whole break observing her and had forgotten to drink his coffee. That knowledge made him feel uncomfortable.

Morgan turned his back on the scene and walked back to his desk, mystified at his actions. It was okay to appreciate a beautiful woman, but to lose time watching her? It wasn't his style. He sat and placed his coffee a safe distance away from the numerous papers, and reminded himself that he was meeting Mary tonight.

Morgan had taken Mary out regularly before he went to London. Sweet, sweet, likeable Mary. He felt that knot of tension again and tried to force it aside. Morgan enjoyed her company, it would be hard not to, but to his regret, he never wanted anything permanent. His ease with her marred by the fact both sets of families assumed he would marry her when the time was right. Before he left for London, he started to feel pressure from all sides, especially when the look in her eyes indicated she wanted more, too.

Almost running away, and feeling like a cad to Mary, he left for London to escape. He said it was because he wanted to study accountancy, but he could do that in Swansea. When he looked back, Morgan knew it was because he was too young to deal with his father's constant demands, as well as a relationship. But, whatever happened all those years ago, Morgan still felt guilty now. Hence, the reason he agreed to take Mary out when his father suggested it. He hoped now he was older, a spark might be there.


Everyone tried to ignore the bell, they were happy chatting.

"Come on, back to work! Your break has finished," shouted the floor supervisor above the noise of the machines.

The workers groaned as they slowly shifted back to work.

Under lowered lashes, Ria glanced at the window that overlooked the work floor. Throughout her break, she had a strange feeling, tingling through her blood. She pretended that the man she saw this morning had been watching her. She knew she was being whimsical, but it made her feel good to dream. Her thoughts brightened her dreary day making clothes.

Ria refused to look up at the one-way window, only giving discrete glances. If he was watching, she wasn't going to give him the satisfaction of looking towards him. If he wasn't watching, it didn't matter.

She felt a shudder move through her, as she moved away from the canteen area, back to her machine. Regardless of what Marge had said earlier, a little romantic dreaming to help the day along never did anyone any harm.

At last, the bell rang to signal the end of the day.

A day with her hair tucked under her hat usually led to a headache if not released, so the first thing Ria routinely did was to untie it. Her curly copper hair tumbled down past her shoulders, as she flicked it with her hands. "Oh, that feels so good." Ria gently rubbed her temples to release the tension where the hair had been pulled tight in its braid.

"I'm glad today is over with. What are you up to tonight, Ria?" Sally inquired while she hung up her overalls in the narrow locker.

"Nothing exciting. I'm going home to help Mam with the cooking."

"Is John coming to walk you home?"

"Yes. Are you up to anything?"

"No." Sally turned away, trying not to let Ria see the envy in her eyes.

Morgan had enough for his first day. He rubbed his hand over the back of his neck, trying to get rid of the tension he could feel there. Pushing away from the desk, that was now piled high with more paperwork to work systematically through, he realised how silent the factory was. Andrew had left for a meeting a couple of hours ago, and the machines had evidently been shut down.

Too restless for coffee, he decided a stretch of his legs and time away from the office was the best option before he returned to the financial paperwork.

Morgan walked down the office steps, and casually cursed his father for bringing him into the problem. As yet, he hadn't found any discrepancies, and he feared it was going to be a long stay in Swansea.

Midway down the steps, Morgan stopped short. He felt his breath had stopped too. Never did he expect to see all that glorious hair coming out of a work hat. He watched as the light caused blonde streaks to appear in the copper colour. Morgan's gut clenched. He had a desperate urge to run his fingers through it, to touch, to feel. Before he released his breath and realised what happened, Ria and the other workers had walked across the factory and pushed open the outside door. No one had seen him as they were busy chatting.

John stood outside, leaning against a stone wall. "Hi, babe." He smiled at them all. He pushed off the wall and walked towards Ria. He slid his arms around her waist and winked at Sally over her shoulder. "Did you think of me as many times as I thought of you?"

Ria smiled back at him. She had learned that teasing banter was the easiest way to keep John happy. "Of course. Although to be truthful, I thought of you as many times as I thought about my aching neck."

"Funny."

"But true." She laughed back.

"Let me rub them for you." A cheeky grin spread on his lips before he turned her around and started to rub her shoulders through her coat.

Ria inhaled. John's fingers felt good kneading her aching muscles. She closed her eyes and leaned back into the massage.

With her eyes shut, Ria failed to see Sally watch them, secretly wishing that John would rub her shoulders instead.

Morgan realised that the workers had left. Just how long had he been standing there? He shook his head, baffled. A simple attraction was easy enough to understand and appreciate. He had, after all, enjoyed many healthy relationships with the opposite sex. But to be rendered senseless by a woman? He quickly rubbed his hands over his face. Perhaps it was the long day that made his thoughts a little strange?

Once he'd calmed and pulled his thoughts together, he realised he had a strong urge to speak to her. Hoping if he got close enough to see her properly or even have a chat, it might answer why she had kept intruding into his mind all day.

As quickly as he could, he made his way across the factory floor, avoiding all the debris that the cleaners had yet to clear away. With slight panic, Morgan tried to remember her name. When he did, he rolled his shoulders, agitated to find that he suddenly felt like an inexperienced teenager.

"Um, excuse me Miss Dillwyn…." He cursed. He was too late. The door had shut. With the noise of machines closing down, she had not heard him call her name.

He strode up to the door and looked through the small window. But what he witnessed didn't please him. It felt as though he had been punched in the stomach. A good looking blond man gave her a hug before he turned her around to massage her shoulders. Morgan curled his hands into fists and stuck them in his pockets. He felt agitated. Having an overwhelming urge to hit something just wasn't him!

Confused at his strong reaction, he cursed again. This was ridiculous. He had only seen her this morning!

Quickly, Morgan turned away from the scene. Never in his life had he felt this surge of jealousy, and it was not something was he comfortable with. At all!

With grim features, he went back to the office and closed the door.

## Chapter 3

The factory was abuzz with gossip. Rumours had started to fly. Why was the boss's son in the factory? Why hadn't they been told he was coming? Were there going to be redundancies?

Not understanding how factory gossip could escalate, Morgan hadn't appreciated the attention he would receive. He hadn't even introduced himself. However, after being told by Andrew how the gossip had reached the attention of the supervisors and bosses, he decided to put a stop to all the chatter.

He called a meeting and formally introduced himself. Amongst other things, Morgan explained that he was there was to learn about the family business, and he would not be involved with the day to day running of the factory. There was a visible sigh of relief when he stated there were no redundancies on the horizon.

During the meeting, everyone's attention was on Morgan. This gave Ria the opportunity to watch him while he addressed the staff. Now she was closer to him, she could see that he vivid blue eyes, framed by black eyebrows. She liked the way they moved up when he said something amusing. His cheekbones were pronounced, and his jaw squared with a little stubble. It could have made him look stern, but to

Ria, his look excited her. She assumed he was in his late twenties, early thirties. Suddenly, she felt disheartened. A man of his experience would be interested in someone like her. After a while, she pushed her negative thoughts aside. This attraction wasn't for real, it was purely her romantic fantasies running wild. It didn't matter if they were different because nothing was ever going to come out of it.

When the meeting finished, Ria felt deflated. She knew she was being childish, but it still stung her pride that he'd never look in her direction for the whole meeting. He'd made eye contact with other employees, but never her.

Feeling dispirited, and even a little childish, Ria turned to go back to work. A frown marred her forehead. It was confusing trying to handle these feeling that she'd never experienced before. She'd never been so attracted to anyone and was unsure whether the feelings would disappear quickly or not. She hoped they did, fancying someone you worked with could be a headache. As she returned to her machine, she decided to have a chat with Karen, her friend. Karen had plenty of experience with men, and she might be able to help to get her emotions back on an even keel.

Morgan finished his speech and watched as the employees returned to work. He was satisfied that there would be no more gossip and that he'd put their concerns about losing their jobs to rest.

As they returned to their machines, Morgan watched a particular red-head. While he'd addressed the employees, he'd found it unbelievably hard not to sought her out. But, she had him feeling like an inexperienced teenager, stumbling for words, so he'd deliberately not looked at her as he didn't want to be distracted from his thoughts.

Morgan though he'd seen an unhappy look on her face when she'd turned away. His eyes narrowed, and his hand rubbed his chin. That was interesting as she usually looked so happy. Had she'd noticed he didn't look at her? Did she care? He felt his mood lighten, secretly hoping she was affected by him, as much as he was affected by her. And boy, was he affected by her.

Since that first day he'd seen her, she was constantly on his mind. Even his date with Mary hadn't dimmed his attraction with Ria. Knowing that wasn't fair to Mary, he'd decided to attempt to forget Ria. But, so far that hadn't helped. He watched her every break time from the window. Stalking wasn't his thing, so he needed to work out what he was going to do. One way or the other.

# Chapter 4

"You look beautiful, my darling." Megan wiped tears from her eyes when Ria walked into the living room.

Ria twirled to show off the dress she'd bought for the work's Christmas party. Feeling beautiful, she walked over and gave her mum an enormous hug. "Thanks, Mam."

Megan stepped back and looked her daughter up and down. Megan sighed. Her daughter looked ladylike in the silver dress. Ria had piled up her hair and clipped it with the silver coloured pins she had given her.

"What about my makeup? Is it too much?"

Megan stepped forward to inspect it. Ria had more makeup on than usual, accentuating her eyes with a hint of green, and her lips glossed with a dusky rose colour, but she looked beautiful. "No, you've done a good job, Victoria."

"Thanks." Ria was looking forward to the party, in fact, the whole factory had been buzzing about it for weeks.

Luckily, she'd been persuaded by Sally and Karen to go shopping to buy a new dress. She was grateful. Previous years, Ria always made do with borrowing a friend's cast-off. This year, her friends and mother insisted she should buy herself something nice with her wages. Even though she had her mother's permission to treat herself, poor Karen and Sally still had to spend ages persuading her to buy it. Now she was wearing it, Ria knew she was going to treasure these feeling, forever.

While Megan cooed and fussed over her, Ria recalled her shopping trip with Karen and Sally. When Karen saw her walk out of the changing room, she'd joked that John would need his father's help to stabilise his blood pressure. Ria had laughed at her joke, but it wasn't John she wanted to affect, but Morgan!

Morgan had been at the factory for months now, but her feelings hadn't diminished. In fact, they had grown. Increased to the point where she couldn't get him out of her mind. At all.

Originally, Ria had planned to confide in Karen and Sally, but for unexplainable reasons, she wasn't ready to share her feelings with them. But Ria reasoned it was partially due to John and partly due to all the gossip surrounding the Templeton men and their reputations.

Ria had mixed feelings about the factory gossip. At times, she enjoyed it, after all, you had to have a certain tolerance for gossip if you worked at a plant. But, on the flip side, Ria knew that gossip had the ability to make someone's life hell. So, as a result,

Ria kept her fantasies to herself, enjoying them without the chance of getting hurt.

Pulling herself out of her thoughts, she twirled once again.

"It falls so nicely," said her mother.

"Yes, it's the material." She grabbed some of the silver material. "It's so soft."

"There's not a lot of it, though," her mother mentioned.

Ria laughed. There wasn't, her back was bare. She craned her neck to see the back of the dress, that draped away to her waist. She remembered with a giggle that Sally told her that wearing a bra would not be an option. At first, Ria had been shocked to find such a revealing dress, especially as most of the clothes being sold were belted at the waist with big skirts. But after some encouragement from her friends, Ria found that she wanted to stand out and look different. But now the time was nearly here, her confidence wavered. She held her breath. She certainly felt wonderful, but would she be able to carry the dress off?

"Those silver heeled shoes are lovely too," Megan said, pulling Ria out of her thoughts.

"Yes, Karen lent them to me."

"You look so lovely, my darling," said Megan as she whipped away a tear of happiness.

"Aw, Mam," replied Ria. Giddy with rollercoaster

emotions, she felt her pulse race with anticipation of the upcoming night. To steady herself, she inhaled a large breath and tried to get her eagerness under control.

Would Morgan notice her? In fact, would he notice her at all? He certainly hadn't shown any interest in her during work.

*Oh, please make him notice me!*

Ria silently reprimanded herself when her emotions plummeted again. Lately, she knew her mood reflected what she was thinking about him, but she couldn't help herself. She knew he was out of her league, and out of her age bracket, but her mind still insisted on internal debates about the possibilities. Realistically, Ria knew the gossip alone should put paid to any interest she had in him, but it didn't. And she certainly didn't want to be used and discarded like the other poor girl, but that didn't stop her emotions either.

"One more twirl, Victoria."

Ria grabbed her skirt and turned. During her Pirouette, Ria decided that tonight was all about enjoying herself, and forgetting her turbulent emotions.

Ria heard the door open. It was her Dad. She held her breath waited nervously for his reaction. Ria thought she saw first pride race across his face, but a stern expression quickly replaced it. "Who did you say you were going out with tonight, Ria?"

Ria bit back a smile, knowing he was being protective. "Why, John…"

His eyes snapped up to look at her.

"…as well as Karen and Sally, and a whole roomful of workers."

Evan knew when his daughter was teasing him. "Ay, well make sure you stay with your friends and… wear a coat. You will catch a cold wearing that handkerchief," he mumbled under his breath as he walked over a gave her a hug, mindful of not messing her hair and makeup. He stepped back and put his hands on her bare shoulders. "Go on, babe. Go and have fun."

"I will."

"Not too much fun, mind," Evan grumbled.

"Evan!" Megan laughed at her husband.

When Ria heard the knock on the front door, she pulled on her coat. Luckily for once, it wasn't her frayed work coat. It was a silver, woollen coat that Sally had lent her for the evening. It was beautiful and finished off her look perfectly. Walking over to them, Ria kissed her parents goodbye. "See you later. Don't wait up."

"We will," said her father as he watched her leave the room, laughing.

Ria opened the door and stepped out into the brisk December night. "Hiya."

"Wow, three beautiful girls to accompany me tonight. I must have done something right in my previous life to deserve this," exclaimed John.

Karen, Sally and Ria laughed.

Sally carefully watched John's reaction when Ria joined them. She saw the look of desire that clouded his eyes. With a sigh, Sally forced a smile and grabbed Ria's and John's arms. "Come on guys. Let's get the party started!"

The Christmas party was in full swing when Ria, John, Sally, and Karen walked through the double doors. Balloons, decorations and lights filled the room. The noise and music sounded loud, but no one seemed to mind.

The four of them lined up to put their coats in the cloakroom. Once they had exchanged their coats for tickets, Ria scanned the room. She didn't kid herself. Ria knew she was searching for Morgan.

She was excited at the prospect of seeing him, but she couldn't find him anywhere. Perhaps he hadn't bothered to come? She felt disappointment creep into her, but she was determined that his attendance, or not, was not going to affect her evening. She had invited John as her plus one, so it wasn't fair to him if she was moody. Ria smiled at her friends. "It's great, isn't it?"

They smiled back.

Both Karen and John took complimentary drinks off a passing tray.

John handed one to Ria. "Looks like the party started without us."

"Thanks," she said.

John looked around. "Let's find a table to put our drinks down. Then I can dance with this beautiful woman in front of me," he said to Ria.

Karen and Sally rolled their eyes.

Ria smiled at John, not the least bit affected by his compliment. She hadn't even felt a flutter of excitement when his eyes practically came out of their sockets when she removed her coat to put in the cloakroom. However, the thought of seeing Morgan sent waves of anticipation and excitement through her.

Once they had settled at the table, her eyes scanned the room again. She tried not making it obvious that she was looking for him.

*Is he here? What if he doesn't come?*

She shook her head. Of course he would come. It was his family's factory. Ria took in another steadying breath and tried to control the buzzing in her brain while pretending to listen to her friend's chit-chat.

Ria took a sip of her drink to calm her nerves. She nearly spilled when John grabbed her elbow.

"There's a bigger table over there," he said as he nodded towards the corner.

Ria glanced towards it, not sure if she wanted to move. The table was a little too in the shadows for her liking.

"Come on. Let's move before someone else snags it," said Karen.

"Okay." Ria knew she was being silly. Her friends were with her, so John wasn't going to try anything untoward.

As she walked over, hoping that nothing spilled onto her new dress, a tingle flitted through her.

Turning her head sharply, Ria glanced towards the shadows. She couldn't see Morgan, but all her senses told her that he was there.  She searched the darkness and saw him far back in the shadows. He seemed to be staring at her, while bending down listening to a petite blonde, whispering into his ear.

Ria hesitated. The smile that had started on her lips stopped. She kicked herself, knowing that someone like Morgan would bring an attractive date. It shouldn't matter, but Ria was annoyed that the blonde looked good in the peach dress that hugged all her delicate curves.  Dejected, but suddenly glad that she'd blown her wages on *her* dress, Ria gave him a quick nod of acknowledgment.  She turned away and caught an amused smile on his face.  She didn't turn back towards him but continued to the table. Once again, he'd unsettled her. Was he amused by her lukewarm reaction or the conversation he was having with the blonde lady?

Morgan and Mary arrived early before the party had started.  His father had reminded him of his duty to be there prematurely, just in case there were problems that needed solving. There hadn't been.

After a brief appearance, his parents had left, hinting heavily that they were leaving 'the youngsters' to enjoy themselves.  Morgan had felt a ripple of annoyance at the blatant attempt at matchmaking.  But, he didn't comment. Besides, Mary was pleasant company, and he had asked her to be his plus one.

So far, Morgan had done his duty, as his father put it.  He'd greeted and chatted employees, helped move furniture, even blew up some balloons, all the while waiting for Ria to arrive.

Morgan knew the moment she walked through the doors. He'd carried on listening to Mary while he watched Ria scan the room.

*Was she looking for him?*

He hoped so. He wanted her to think of him as much as he thought of her.

He'd decided, after lying awake night after night, that even though she was younger than him, worked for his family, and might not have any interest in him, he needed to find out whether she was interested in him. He was determined to find out. For his sanity.

When she'd arrived, it had taken all his strength not to make his feelings obvious to those around him when she'd removed her coat. All she had on was a silver dress, which skimmed her body in all the right places. Morgan became too hot under the collar for comfort. She was even more beautiful out of her work overall. Her copper coloured hair was up and secured with shiny clips that reflected the lights in the room. He preferred it down, but it suited the dress she was wearing.

Morgan was grateful for the loud music because it masked his curse from Mary. When Ria turned around to get a drink from the blond man, and her back was completely exposed. Uncomfortable, Morgan suddenly realised that he might not be the only red-blooded man in the party to notice her. It wasn't something he liked very much.

When he realised that Mary was speaking to him, due to the noise, he bent down to hear her. But, he was still unable to take his eyes off Ria.

Morgan's stomach clenched when he watched her smile at her date. He recognised him as the man giving her a massage at the factory. He cursed the 'plus one' invitations. While he half listened to Mary, Ria finally glanced over at him. Their gazes locked.  Morgan felt his pulse surge. It amused him when Ria's gaze flicked over Mary, and then gave him a curt nod. She seemed to be annoyed. Morgan smiled.

Perhaps she was affected by him after all?

All he needed now was an opportunity to find out!


Ria loved dancing.  The moves, the bump of bodies, the laughs, the smiles, the energy. It made her feel alive. Invigorated.

Although she spent most of the evening dancing with John and her friends, Ria still couldn't forget that Morgan was around. In fact, she hoped he was watching her because she was a good dancer. She'd been careful to keep an eye on his whereabouts. It added to the high spirits she was experiencing.

While trying to watch him, she'd noticed that Morgan spent most of his evening talking to his date or employees.  He'd not danced at all.  He hadn't looked at her, either.  Deflated again, she berated herself. It was silly to want someone who clearly showed no interest in her. Ria felt as though she was putting on a show of normality when inside she was a mess.

Morgan knew he had to keep talking to people around him. It stopped him thinking or looking at Ria. Usually, there was nothing he liked more than dancing a night away. But, he knew if he went on the dance floor, he would have to get his hands on Ria.

At the beginning of the night, he'd had trouble keeping his eyes off her. Her body had been taunting him. But, it soon became too difficult to see her dancing with her date.  Not a violent man, Morgan was uncomfortable with the fact he wanted to break the arms of her date when he touched her.  So, to counter his emotions, he turned his back on the dance floor and tried to concentrate on Mary and any employees who wanted a chat.

When one song finished and another one started, Ria pushed her hair out of her eyes. She realised that some pins had worked themselves loose.  "Karen, I'm popping to the bathroom to sort my hair out," she shouted over the noise.

"I'll meet you there when this song has finished. It's my favourite," Karen shouted back, before turning and lifting her arms in the air to continue dancing to the song.

Ria laughed and stood watching Karen and Sally dance their way into the middle of the dance floor.  She looked for John and found him getting the drinks at the bar.

Humming the song, and distracted with her thoughts, Ria pushed at the door.

The same time as Morgan.

They bumped into each other.

Morgan looked down at her surprised face. To his delight, he saw a tiny splattering of freckles across her nose. The knots in his stomach that had been playing with him all evening grew even tighter now he was near her. Panicking, Morgan knew he couldn't let her get away easily. Or let this opportunity pass.

He'd never been this close to her before, so his gaze wandered over her face, drinking it in. When he noticed a suspicious look enter her eyes, he silently cursed. Obviously, his scrutiny had been too intense. "Sorry," he said. He coughed when he noticed how thick his voice had become.

A nervous smile flickered on Ria's lips. "It's okay. I didn't see you either," she said, misunderstanding what he was sorry about.

When he noticed her eyes flick towards the door, panic hit him when he thought she was going. His desire kicked in and overrode all his senses. He glanced around, and silently blessed the people who had decorated the room, with Christmas in mind. He knew he shouldn't, but he couldn't help himself. He wanted her in his arms.

"Um, I'd better go," Ria said, unsure about the silence that had descended on them.

Morgan nodded upwards. "Look up," he said to her, in an attempt to stop her walking away.

"Mistletoe," he muttered, "and if tradition is to be followed, that means that we need to kiss".

Ria tried to swallow, but her mouth was suddenly dry. There was nothing more she would like than to kiss him! She found the courage to look at him, although she was glad the lights were dim so he wouldn't see her blush.

She so wanted to kiss him.

Reality set in. She shouldn't kiss him. He was with a gorgeous blonde lady and technically, she had come with John.

She glanced at his kissable lips as her mind argued.

*But, he was only asking for a Christmas kiss!*

Morgan couldn't let her back off. He watched her quietly study him, indecision written all over her face. Panic rose within him. He knew he was being unfair, but he had to take the decision away from her.

Taking a step forward, he cornered her against a wall.

The doors gently swung shut, fading the noise out.

Morgan's gaze flittered around her face and landed back on her painted lips. His head slowly moved forward, his lips a whispered breath away. "What do you say? Do you think we should follow tradition?"

"I, um…" *Why wasn't her brain work properly?*

Morgan raised his eyebrows. He needed her to answer. She was killing him. "So?"

"Um," she whispered annoyed at herself. For heaven's sake, she was being silly, making a mountain out of a molehill. He'd only asked for a quick Christmas kiss under the mistletoe.

*Didn't he?*

"I won't kiss you until you agree, Ria."

Her stomach constricted at the sound of her name on his tongue. Pretending to be more confident than she was, she looked deep into his blue eyes. She nearly lost her nerve, when she could tell they were cloudy with desire, but her emotions took over. Ria felt a blush rise. She felt foolish, as he hovered there waiting for her consent. Why couldn't she form a coherent sentence? More importantly, why couldn't she breathe properly? "Yes."

A small smile flickered on Morgan's lips.

The noise from the party was suddenly replaced by the roar of her blood and the pounding of her heart.

Morgan took a step closer, moving his body as near as he dared. He was not giving her any chance of pulling away. As he looked down at her face, he noticed colour appear on her cheeks. It delicately tainted her pale skin. He felt the mighty rush of desire. Taking a small breath to control himself, he knew he couldn't wait any longer. "A Christmas kiss?" he whispered.

"Yes."

The pull was getting too much for him, he couldn't hold out any longer. The thought of kissing the sweet lips that had kept him awake for too many nights was mind-blowing, but he wasn't going to rush her.

Morgan ran his knuckles gently over her cheekbone. He could smell her subtle perfume, it made its way into his bloodstream. He slowly bent his head and gently sampled her lips.

Morgan only intended to give her a Christmas kiss. He wanted it to be good, but it was only going to be brief. Heavens, he was experienced enough to control desire. Even if it was boiling just beneath the surface.

But, she made a mistake. She sighed.

It brought him to his knees.

With a heady weakness he'd never experienced before, he felt the need to taste more of her. With no regard to their surroundings, Morgan gently cupped his hand on the back of her head, bringing her closer. Slowly deepening his kiss, he was delighted when her lips parted slightly in invitation.

That was all the invitation he needed.

As he sampled her mouth, a mixture of both sweet and spicy, he forgot his original intentions. Her pulse that hammered into his palm, her quiet moans that he swallowed, her pliable body pressed up against him, all forced him to grasp tightly onto his last thin line of control.

Initially, when she bumped into him, and he'd asked for a kiss, Ria assumed the kiss was going to be a friendly Christmas peck - one between a boss and worker. When he moved slowly towards her, the look in his eyes told her differently.

But she wanted it.

The initial shock of his lips on hers was electric, but within seconds, his gentle kiss made her melt against him. She barely noticed his large, warm hand cup the back of her neck, pulling her nearer. Little of a coherent nature formed in her mind while her body reacted to the deepening kiss. Squeezing her eyes tight, she attempted to eliminate the nagging little doubt that tried to push, though. She didn't want to listen. Ria wanted to kiss him, but she did not want him to know how inexperienced she was. She hoped he couldn't tell that she was starting to pull away in panic.

Ria's sudden and complete surrender to his kiss had his needs churning to the surface. As his hand moved down her back to pull her closer, he felt a slight tensing in her body. It was all he needed. He realised that his desire had made him go further than he intended.

Cursing in his mind, he summoned all his strength to break their contact. He categorically didn't want to stop and focus on what was right, but he knew he had to be responsible. Before they did something they might regret.

Very carefully, like a man backing away from imminent danger, he stepped away from her.

*Wow, what a kiss.* Was the only thought going through Ria's brain. The taste and smell of him had her senses reeling. But suddenly, he had her standing at arm's length with his hands on her shoulders. He then took a step back and backed off completely.

"Ria," he said in a voice that sounded more composed than he felt.

"Yes?" she whispered. Automatically, she touched her swollen lips. When his gaze narrowed on her fingers, she immediately felt foolish. Her world had not stopped spinning, and he was already pushing her away.

"I'm sorry. That shouldn't have happened."

Embarrassment tore through her. How silly she was to let her feet be swept from beneath. Morgan must have kissed many women before. Her inexperience must have repulsed him. Mortification took hold when she imagined him going back to his blonde bombshell for a laugh. "No, it shouldn't have," she managed to squeak out.

now because he'd consumed a little too much to drink.

Glancing around the room, Ria didn't bother to fool herself that she wasn't looking for Morgan. She couldn't get him out of her mind. Especially since that kiss. He had sent her emotions all over the place, making her buzz with the feelings.

Eventually, she spotted him. Jealousy tore through her and grabbed her heart.

Morgan was putting his date's coat around her shoulders and kissing her forehead.

Confused, Ria looked away.

*Hadn't their kiss affected him at all?*

That hurt. How could he casually kiss his date when she was disturbed by it so much that she was agitated with John when he touched her. Her stomach churned, her emotions all over the place before she became angry.

*How dare Morgan have the gall to carry on as normal!*

Wanting to get some air, Ria turned around abruptly. She landed straight into John's embrace.

"Fancy a cuddle then, babe?" John slurred his words, the amount of drink he had consumed affecting his speech.

Before Ria could remove herself from his roaming arms, a fist connected with John's chin. John smashed into the tables.

"Leave the lady alone! Someone get him out! He's drunk," Morgan shouted.

Ria heard the thread of violence in Morgan's voice, but it didn't compare to the anger that started to bubble within her.

*How dare he!*

She walked towards John, who sat between the upturned tables, clutching his jaw and wiggling it. The alcohol and punch made everything woozy.

"What on earth just happened?" John shook his head to clear it. He narrowed his eyes when he caught sight of Morgan glaring at him while rubbing the knuckles that had apparently hit him. Unaware who he was addressing, John growled. "Ria is with *me!* I've got no idea what *your* problem is, mush, but she has no problems with me touching her!"

Morgan fought to control his temper. "Get him out now!" Morgan stated through clenched teeth. He looked around for the doormen who had run over. Morgan noticed, but ignored, all the stares he was getting. He knew he shouldn't have got involved, but he *was* involved.

*Damn it!*

When the doormen arrived, Morgan looked at Ria. She was kneeling next to the fallen man. She didn't look at him. Envy reared its ugly head, but Morgan forced himself to stay still.

As he stood there, Morgan was forced to realise that he didn't want anyone, apart from himself, to touch Ria. Jealousy wasn't an emotion he was used to, and the power of it made him uncomfortable. But at the moment, as his blood raced through him, there was nothing he could do.

Ria bent down to check on John out. When she knew he was okay, she glanced over her shoulder at Morgan. Morgan was standing still, staring at her. Her green eyes darkened with fury. She didn't know who she was madder with – Morgan or John! "Why you! You... men.  Sorting things out with your fists. You've nothing more than a bunch of animals," she hissed in Morgan's direction.   She turned back towards John. "You, too." She punched a finger into his shoulder.

Annoyed at the look of surprise on John's face, she stood up and turned away from him, towards Morgan. Ria was so angry that they both seemed to think they could decide what she did, she was unaware of the whispers going on around her.  "*I* can say who can touch me *and* when!"

Looking at Ria, Morgan felt the red fog that had controlled him up to now, disappear. He was ashamed of his actions, but he still felt the urge to grab Ria and kiss her in front of everyone.     Morgan turned abruptly from the scene.  He needed to.

There already would be enough gossip in the coming week for them to deal with.

Morgan nodded a curt farewell at those still staring at him and turned to Mary. Forcing his hands to be gentle on her shoulders, he steered her out of the door. As the door started to swing shut, the silence ended, and the hum of gossip started.

They walked into the darkness, and for once, he was glad he was with Mary. She would not ask any questions to rock the boat.

In silence, they walked to the car. Morgan opened the door for Mary, and she quietly slipped into the seat. He walked around the car and got in.

Waiting for Mary to settle, he slid her a brief glance. Her blonde hair glistened in the moonlight. His stomach clenched, but with agony not desire.

He so wished he didn't want the fiery red hair so desperately instead.

Morgan forced himself to relax. Once composed, he turned to Mary and gave her a half-hearted smile. "Okay?"

"Yes."

"Then I'll take you home." He leant forward, turning on the radio. He didn't want to talk.

Apart from the sound from the stereo turned low, the ride home was silent and tense. He was glad when they arrived at Mary's parents' house He needed to be alone. He needed to think.

Quickly, he jumped out and walked around to let her out of the car. Out of habit, Morgan escorted her to the door to say goodnight.

This time, however, there were no sweet kisses under the door light. He kissed her gently on the cheek and said goodnight before turning away.

Morgan didn't witness the tears slowly fall Mary's face - her heart broken.

~~~~

Morgan didn't feel like going home. Despite the late hour, he certainly didn't feel like sleeping, he was too restless.

After driving aimlessly for a while, Morgan found himself driving through back streets, heading towards Ria's house. He knew where she lived. He'd previously checked her information out at work. At the time, he'd pretended that it was necessary to know details about his employees. But, he knew he was lying. It was only Ria's information he sought out.

Just before he reached her street, he stopped the car. He put his elbows on the steering wheel and rubbed his hands over his face. When he closed his eyes, he could see the look in Ria's fiery eyes when she was crouched over John. He blew out an exasperated breath.

He was annoyed with himself, again. He had no right to kiss her so passionately under the mistletoe when she was with someone else. He certainly had no right to kiss her when she had gone to the party with her boyfriend.

Gripping the steering wheel, he winced at the pain in his hands. He looked at his red knuckles.

*What was happening to him?*

He'd never felt so confused before. And he didn't particularly like it.

Morgan sat back and closed his eyes. He attempted to recall the night to try and put things in perspective. He needed to make some sense of what happened, make sense of his actions too.

In reality, he imagined Ria would have expected an ordinary Christmas kiss. Not the one he gave her. After all, she had no idea that he fancied her. Morgan cringed. He was appalled that he lost control and took the kiss further without even asking her. It wasn't like him at all.

*Perhaps she hadn't wanted more than a peck?*
*But her body responded.*

Morgan shook his thoughts away. Other than the occasional polite salutation when they passed each other, they hadn't spoken until tonight. Ria could have been afraid to tell him she didn't want him to kiss her. He was the boss's son, after all.

Morgan pushed back into the car seat. He covered his eyes with his arm, his stomach clutched with anxiety. It didn't matter how she responded to his kiss. He was experienced enough to know that was just her body, not her mind, reacting to him. She might not even like him.

Morgan knew he needed to talk to her. Or forget about her.

He just didn't know which road to take.

A while later, after searching for answers, and not finding many, Morgan's energy disappeared. He leant forward onto the steering wheel.

He felt hopeless, but he was in the wrong. He had never poached a woman off someone else, and he wasn't going to start now. Ria already had a boyfriend, so he *had* to keep away from her.

Even though he didn't want to.

Morgan ground his jaw tightly. He flicked the car ignition back on and drove away from her street.

## Chapter 5

*Men are idiots! The lot of them!*

Ria strode along the shoreline of the beach, her silver shoes dangling in her fingers. Even though it was winter, and the sand was icy cold, she didn't care. The massaging sand soothed her feet that were aching from dancing.

After Morgan and his blonde girlfriend left, Ria asked Sally and Karen to walk John home. He was in no fit state to get home without help. Ria hadn't wanted to go with them because she needed time to sort her head out. Besides, as soon as she got home, her parents and siblings would question her about the night and she didn't need that. She was too confused.

In the moonlight, Ria continued to walk the empty beach, devoid of everything except hollow footprints. Stopping, she watched her feet sink into the cold, damp sand. She was all alone but didn't feel lonely. The familiarity of the beach calmed her.

Turning towards the sea, Ria watched the violent waves. She signed. Her insides felt like that at the moment. As she watched the white horses race across the sea, she allowed her mind to wander to the evening's events.

*What a night. What a mess.*

She was annoyed at both John and Morgan.
*Why did they behave like that?*

The drink had made John touchier with her, he wasn't normally like that. And Morgan, she realised with a sigh, she didn't know Morgan's personality at all. Apart from a hello in work, she hadn't spoken to him.

*But that kiss.*

That kiss was *so* different to anything she had experienced before. But, as a consequence, she didn't know how to handle it or the after effects. Ria knew her body had reacted, and that she'd enjoyed it, but in reality, she didn't have a clue what Morgan wanted from her. Did he see her as a worker that he could have fun with before returning to his blonde girlfriend? Were people of his social class able to 'mess around' with the minions before marrying someone of the same wealth? Was there more truth in Marge-the-gossip's words about the Templeton men than Ria was willing to admit?

Closing her eyes tight against the breeze, Ria sighed deeply. One thing was for sure, she needed to talk to John. It was unfair to string him along, now she realised that she felt entirely different about his kisses and Morgan's.

Ria didn't know how long she stood, eyes closed, listening to the sea, but, after a while, a strange sensation fluttered through her. It had nothing to do with the frigid air. She knew Morgan was behind her. She could feel him there, even though the noise of the waves had drowned out the sound of an approaching car.

Refusing to turn, Ria took in calming breaths and continued to look at the waves.

At first, Morgan couldn't believe it was her. He took a minute to make sure, but it was! No one could mistake that gloriously coloured hair.

*Damn, what do I do?*

Unsure, Morgan stood. He watched her hair dancing in the wind, and the waves roaring in front her. She was still. He, however, felt like his blood was mimicking the sea.

He shoved his hands in his pocket. Unsure of his next move.

*Did she know he was here?*

Morgan winced with pain when his knuckles brushed his pocket. It abruptly reminded him of what went on that evening. A thread of fear ran through him.

*What would he do if she told him to go away?*

Regardless of his fears, the urge to walk over and touch her was overwhelming. In the end, whether she wanted him there or not, he couldn't stop his feet walking towards her.

It took all of Ria's strength to turn around to look at him because she knew that once she did, there would be no going back. Her heart fluttered as she watched him walk over the sand towards her.

As Morgan made his way nearer to her, his face was impassive, not giving any secrets away. But his insides were anything but.

"Hello," he said when he reached her. He looked into her green eyes, trying to read her emotions. She didn't look angry with him anymore. He breathed a sigh of relief.

In the dim light, she looked at him. He seemed unsure of what to do. He was nothing like the confident, angry man who was at the party.

The turbulent waters roared, and the frigid air swirled around them, but between them, everything was still.

Eventually, Morgan broke the silence. "I'm sorry about your partner. I don't know what came over me." He shook his head but never broke eye contact with her. "I haven't behaved like that since I was a teenager." He took a steadying breath, unable to carry on.

Ria started to speak but stopped when Morgan put his hand up so he could finish what he wanted to say.

"I've realised it was wrong to kiss you."

Her mood deflated.

"You were at the party with someone else. Your boyfriend. I have no excuses, but let me assure you…" His words stuck in his throat. "It will not happen again." He finished his admission firmly, trying to convince himself as much as her.

Ria felt the tension flow out of her. He was sorry, not about kissing her, but because he thought John was her boyfriend. And, at least, he was prepared to apologise.

"Oh."

"Oh?" His eyes narrowed on her.

Ria smiled slowly and took a step towards him. "So you are sorry about my *boyfriend*, you behaved like a *teenager*, you were wrong to *kiss* me, and it will not *happen* again?" She lifted her eyebrow and noticed he looked uncomfortable, uncertain. Until tonight, she'd only seen him control before, and the thought that she had the ability to affect him was a heady sensation.

"Yes," he murmured, shifting uneasily. Ria seemed to be playing a game with him. Her face was flushed, and she had a twinkle in her eye. But, what was her end game? He quickly broke off the intense eye contact and looked towards the sea before he did something foolish – again.

"Yes?"

Her question prompted him to look back at her. On the wind, he caught her smell. She smelled so good. Her, mixed with a hint of the salty sea air had his blood stirring again. Calming himself, he noticed the playful smile on her full lips. The lips he wanted to kiss again. She was flirting with him. Flirting was something he could deal with.

Morgan cocked his head to the side. Now he realised she wanted to play, it cleared his uncertainties away. The thrill spread warmly through his veins. "Or no?"

Morgan chuckled when her eyes widened. Carefully, in an attempt not to spook her playfulness, he raised his arm and gently ran his knuckles along her cheekbone. He hoped she didn't detect the tremor in his hand. His nervousness and excitement were all too apparent to him.

Gently, he tipped her chin up, to enable him to look straight into her eyes. When she didn't pull away, and he saw no negative signs, his other hand captured the back of her neck. His thumb moved in slow circular motions over her rapidly beating pulse.

*Oh, gosh! That feels so good.*

Morgan observed her responses to his touch. He had promised himself he would stop at the first indication that she wanted to her. To his joy, he noticed her eyes glass with desire, before they fluttered shut. Morgan wanted to shout his happiness from the rooftops, but he kept his composure calm.

Morgan leant forward an inch and stopped, waiting for her reaction. His mouth was so close to hers, their breath mingled in the air.  He only had to lean in to claim her lips, and although it cost him, he kept a clamp on his emotions.  "No, I will not kiss you again until you ask me," he whispered.

Ria's eyes flew open.

Morgan saw disappointment flick through them. He needed to be sure what she wanted. As they stood in silence, an unexpectedly felt an overwhelming urge of possession grip him.  "I will *only* kiss you when you are *only* kissing me.  No one else."  He realised that he had never asked someone to be exclusively his. But the hard fact was, he wanted Ria to be his. Only his.

Ria tried to process what he said.

*Did he mean that he wanted her? For what? Girlfriend or lover?*

Waiting for a response was killing Morgan. He was working hard at being level headed enough for the both of them. He needed a commitment from her. For Ria to get rid of her boyfriend. He couldn't deny that he did badly want to kiss her sweet lips, but he also recognised that when he was around her, he lost his self-control.  "What do you think, Ria?"

He looked at her desperately wanting her to answer. She didn't. And to make matter worse, she looked confused. For his sanity, he needed to regain control. He knew it would take little effort to get her to kiss him. But, he wanted her to make the next move. "Ria?" he whispered, but still got no response.

Morgan understood that he needed to get away from temptation. Before he forgot his promise of self-control.

"Goodnight, Ria." With all his strength, he turned and started to walk away.

*He's leaving. I don't want him to.* Ria shook the confused thoughts out of her head. "Morgan."

Morgan stopped and let out the breath he had been holding.

"There is no one else," Ria whispered at his retreating back, desperate for him to come back.

Morgan turned around slowly. *Play it cool*, he kept repeating in his mind. Forcing himself to go slowly, he made his way back to her. As he walked, he watched the wind whip up strands of her hair across her pale face, her eyes huge with expectation. She looked so beautiful.

Even though it was only a couple of steps, it felt like an eternity until he reached her. When he did, Morgan reached out with both hands to tenderly cradle her face. When Ria looked up at him through half-closed lashes, he relaxed. She wanted him, too. However, this time, he would use as much control as he could muster. During their previous kiss, he recognised that she wasn't as experienced as him. He didn't want to make her run, he would treat her with kid gloves.

Ria shuddered at Morgan's contact. His hands were warm compared to the cold air that swirled around her. She stared into his blue eyes, and her body naturally swayed into him. It felt as though her bones had melted, and her legs had turned to liquid.

"Ask me, Ria. Ask me to kiss you," he whispered.

"Yes. Yes… kiss me," she whispered back. When her fingers curled around the lapels of his overcoat, her shoes quietly dropped onto the sand.

It was all the encouragement he needed. Her mouth was soft and warm. He traced the outline of her lips with his tongue. When he felt her shiver beneath his hands, he proceeded to place soft kisses on her face until he could feel her relax. Totally. His tongue wanted nothing more than to invade her sweet mouth, but he resisted the urge to move too fast. He was going to take it painfully slow.

All thoughts slipped out of her mind as Ria concentrated on the pleasure being released through her body. His experienced kisses spread a fire through every part of her. A warm, tight feeling pooled low in her stomach. With a shiver, she swayed nearer to his solid chest. Her hands moved up to pull him towards her mouth. She wanted him to kiss her. She needed him closer.

He complied.

Never before had Ria felt the myriad of emotions swirl through her bloodstream. Her relaxed brain didn't allow her to dissect and analyse it. She was going with the flow and liked where it was taking her. The previous tension of uncertainty that had caused a tight ball of anxiety in her stomach, diminished to make way for an altogether different sensation. It was an incredible feeling. She wanted more of it.

Morgan wanted more of her, to taste more of her. He changed the angle of his head to take his feather-like kisses into deeper ones. When her body become more pliable, and a moan escaped her lips, he realised just how well her body fit against his. He felt her pull him closer, her actions played havoc with him. "Ria," he murmured against her cheek.

"Morgan," she replied, breathlessly.

Morgan curled his fingers through her loose hair. Tilting her head back to get better access. The need to invade her sweet mouth heated his body. As he delved, he didn't know if it was the roar of the waves, or his blood, that he could now hear. He wanted her. His hunger for her increasing, he pulled her body as close as he could to the hard contours of his. He filled his hands with her curves as his mouth devoured hers.

In a brief instant of clarity, he realised that Ria was matching his desire and passion. She was kissing him

back as vigorously as he kissed her. She wasn't
backing away.

*Perhaps she wasn't inexperienced after all?*
*Perhaps he'd been wrong?*

A thrill shot through him. He didn't need to take it
slow. And, if he played his cards right, perhaps she
would come home with him?

Morgan's hand moved down her back, pressing
her as near as possible. He wondered whether she
could feel his excitement as he deepened his kiss, his
tongue playing with hers.

He certainly could.

Angling his body, his hand sought out the front of
her coat, needing to get rid of the barrier between
them. Slowly, he undid the coat buttons. A groan
rumbled deep in his chest. Only a thin piece of silver
dress separated them, the fine material a weak
barrier against the sensations of his hard
embrace. "Ria," he murmured, before claiming her
mouth again.

Moving closer, his hand slipped inside the parted
coat. His hand stopped its exploration. His thumb
brushed the underside of her breast and through the
haze he realised she did not have a bra on.

*How much more could he take?*

Cupping her breast through the material, he
swallowed Ria's moan. She nearly sent him over the
edge when she instinctively pushed against his hand.

He moved his hand away. He was going too fast. Instead, his hand searched for the naked back that had tormented him throughout the evening. "Damn, Ria. You're so beautiful."

"Hmmm." Ria sought out his lips again. She didn't want words, they would bring reality back. She wanted kisses and touch. They made her melt. Made her feel like she was fluid, drowning in a calm sea of sensations.

With desire taking hold, Ria stopped listening to his whispered endearments. Her brain was too fuzzy. She was totally lost in the moment, even forgetting they were on a public beach. The way her body was responding, Ria was oblivious to everything and everyone, other than themselves.

"Do you want to go come back to mine? We'll be more comfortable there."

Ria pulled away slightly. "Pardon?"

"I said, do you want to come back to mine?"

His words were like a bucket of cold water, breaking the spell. The fog of desire started to clear and Ria began to panic.

*Of course! Of course! How silly to get carried away. What was I thinking?*

She shook her head.

"What's wrong, Ria?" Morgan said his brow furrowing.

Panicking, she tried to break out of his gentle hold, putting her hands on his chest to push him back. As his warm hand left her back, she shuddered. She now felt the cold, outside and in.

"What's wrong?" His eyes narrowed onto her trembling lip. "Tell me, please."

Words wouldn't form through her humiliation. Tears glazed her eyes.

*Hadn't she been warned that he would be after one thing? One thing only!*

Marge's words sprang to mind. '*Mind you, he won't get too close to us mere workers. Oh no, well perhaps only for slap and tickle.*'

Mortification shot through her, and Ria trembled. *They were right!*

Morgan panicked as he felt Ria withdraw. It was the last thing he wanted.

*What had he said?*

He watched as she averted her eyes awkwardly from him. He'd told her that he fancied her, he'd told her that he wanted to see her. What had upset her? He pushed his hand through his hair. How could he get her to tell him what was wrong? "Ria, please."

Rai stepped back until they were no longer touching. Suddenly feeling the cold, she wrapped her coat firmly around her. She needed to say something, but what?

Anger was the only way Ria could think to deal with the situation. She certainly didn't want Morgan to know how naive she felt! Having feelings for him when his were clearly not the same type. She forced herself to look him in the eye. Ignoring the confused look on his face, she lashed out. "Is that the kind of girl you think I am?" she accused while feeling sick to her stomach. "One you can charm into your bed, and then dump, no doubt?"

"What?" Morgan took a step forward in an attempt to calm her down. He stopped when she shook her head.

"Well I'm not, and I'm sorry if that kiss gave you any other ideas." Ria pulled the front of the coat more tightly around her, the chill suddenly coursing through her. Her eyes narrowed for a couple of seconds, daring him to reply.

Morgan stood still, trying to gather his thoughts. *What just happened?*

Feeling her anger drain away, she knew she needed to go. If she stayed, she was petrified that she would be that type of girl. Turning quickly, she headed away walking as fast as she could in the sand.

"Ria?"

"Ria," he said louder at her retreating back. "Don't go."

She heard him call. But she didn't stop. The humiliation of all her responses stung too much for her to return.

Morgan stood in the sand, confused. He had always felt comfortable around women, so how on earth did this one turn him inside out? What did he keep doing wrong? Why was he so bad at reading her signals?

Morgan called out to her again, but she ignored him and kept on walking. He rubbed his hand over his chin.

Perhaps he had read her signals wrong?

She was much younger than him, and initially he'd thought she would be inexperienced. He had respected that. But that kiss! There was nothing unsophisticated about that! It had made his blood stir in all the right places.

As confusion clouded his thoughts, his temper reared its head, too. A strange feeling clawed at his stomach. He didn't like it.

*He would have never asked her to sleep with him if he thought it would offend her. He wasn't that type of man!*

His face flushed.

*Wasn't he whispering endearments into her ear? Ria didn't seem to have any objections to what he was saying then!*

He pushed his clenched fists into his pockets.

*So why did she change so much?*

Morgan stood and watched as she disappeared into the darkness. He glanced up and down the deserted beach. Turning towards the sea, he took a deep breath of the fresh, salty air, and closed his eyes. Morgan shook his head and cursed when it became apparent that part of his anger was directed at himself - for frightening her enough to make her run away. It was the last thing he wanted.

He didn't want her to go, but it didn't look as though he had a choice. Sighing, he decided to follow her home. To make sure she was safe.

As Morgan leant against the street lamp, he watched the light in her bedroom go on. As far as he could tell, she hadn't known he'd followed her. She hadn't let him know, anyway.

His jaw clenched as he imagined her getting ready for bed. The image was too vivid for comfort.

He exhaled noisily.

*Just when did he let a woman get to him? When did a woman ever get under his skin? How could someone he just met unleash such strong feelings?*

He was baffled. He'd thought he had enough experience to know what a woman wanted. But, this copper-headed lady just had him feeling like a thoughtless oaf when he was around her.

His confusion and vulnerability rapidly turned into annoyance, again. It annoyed him that he thought of her when he was supposed to be doing paperwork. It annoyed him when he looked forward to breaktime so he could watch her laugh with her friends. And, it certainly annoyed him that he felt emotionally unstable. Whether Ria knew it or not, she was playing with his head!

Glancing back at her house, he noticed the bedroom light eventually switch off. Morgan turned and walked away, determined that he would get her out of his system. One way or another.

## Chapter 6

"Morgan, the phone is for you," Nell, his mother, called.

"Okay, I'll be there now."

Nell's eyes narrowed when she watched her son walk to the phone. It was obvious that something was bothering him. Being a light sleeper, she also noticed that he spent the last two nights pacing his room because his movements disturbed her.

As he neared, Nell saw he had echoes of shadows under his eyes, highlighting his lack of rest. She handed him the receiver, and he gave her a tight smile of thanks.

Nell turned away. If she thought about it, lately, Morgan was either quiet or cranky with everyone. She smiled. Ever the romantic, Nell came to the conclusion that her son must have had a disagreement with Mary. He'd been touchy since the Christmas party. If he was this affected by an argument with Mary, it must mean that she was very special to him. With Nell's mind on overdrive, she rushed over to her husband, who was reading the sporting section of the newspaper. "David."

"Yes, love?" David replied, looking over the top of his paper.

As Morgan put the receiver to his ear, he vaguely watched his mother. She was whispering into his father's ear. Not interested, Morgan turned his back on them and listened to his flatmate, Ted, on the other end.

"Was anything stolen? Is there much damage? Yes, of course, I will leave this afternoon and be with you by this evening. Okay, see you later. Bye."

Morgan turned from the phone. A frown marred his forehead. This was something he didn't need to complicate his life at the moment. He was stressed enough with the Ria situation.

"Everything alright, Morgan?" his mother asked.

"No." He silently cursed as he rubbed his face.

"What's wrong, son?" said David.

"There had been a robbery at my London apartment."

"Oh no," said Nell, her hands grasped at her chest.

"Ted doesn't think anything had been taken because the burglars were disturbed."

"Oh, that's good." Nell gave a slight smile.

Morgan rubbed the back of his neck. "But the police are insisting that I return to check my belongings." This was the last thing he felt like doing, travelling to London after nights of insomnia. He looked at his mother's worried expression.

*Perhaps fate was playing its hand?*

Suddenly, Morgan realised it might do him good to get away. He would have some space to think. He knew if he saw Ria in work before he worked out what he wanted, she would end up messing with his head again! Morgan made up his mind. "Mum, Dad. I'm going to London for the week."

"What about the factory?" David questioned his son.

Morgan tried to hide his wry smile. Of course, the factory was always the top priority. "It's okay. I'll ring Andrew Jones and explain why I will be away."

His father nodded, before returning to read his paper.

"Don't worry. I won't be gone long," he said to soothe his mother.

When he turned to make his way into the study, Morgan missed his mother's calculating smile.

"Quick, David. Use the private line," she nudged his arm in an attempt to stop him reading. "Ring Mary and ask if she would like to go up to London with Morgan." She tapped her chin. "Darren can go too. He mentioned to me that he wanted to pop up to London to catch up with his friends."

When David didn't move, she waved her arms to hurry her husband along. He was going far too slow. Morgan might find out what she was up to before they rang Mary. "That older boy of ours needs a bit of a push to know what is right for him."

David heaved a heavy sigh at his wife's antics. He, himself, liked to dabble in a bit of matchmaking - what father wouldn't like to see his sons married and producing heirs?  But his wife certainly gave him a run for his money.

~~~~

Morgan pushed down on the accelerator. Tension flowed through him as his hands tightened his grip on the steering wheel.

*How on earth did both Mary and his brother end up coming to London?*

Morgan wanted time to think about his life, not to entertain his brother and Mary. He wasn't happy.

When he finally drove onto the main road to London, Morgan became aware of the quiet atmosphere within the car. Apparently, both his passengers were picking up on his mood. Morgan took a deep breath. It certainly wasn't Mary's fault he was feeling so wound up about Ria. Mary shouldn't be sat next to him, nervously entwining her fingers, a hurt look on her face. Why was he so annoyed that Mary was here? His brother wasn't going to be an inconvenience either. Darren would be off to catch up with his friends.

Morgan turned his head towards Mary to start a conversation. Anything to lighten the atmosphere.

After a while, everyone relaxed and made small talk.

The journey to London was long. Darren, who had been out with his friends the previous evening, had fallen asleep in the back. Mary quietly looked out of the side window.

The lull in conversation allowed Morgan's mind to drift towards Ria.

During the last couple of days, Morgan had accepted that Ria was under his skin. Well and truly. Whether she was near him or not, she had the ability to affect him.

Morgan knew he wanted her, but after rethinking the events, he came to the conclusion his actions had been wrong - his treatment of her, and his subsequent anger. It was obvious now that Ria wasn't experienced, and therefore, he'd been totally out of order expecting her to sleep with him. Although he still wanted her, he had no idea what her values were. He couldn't assume a local girl would have the same attitude to sex as one from London.

Morgan glanced over at Mary, who still gazed out of the window. To be honest, Ria's innocence frightened him. Years before, he had taken Mary's innocence. And, truthfully, he'd felt indebted since.

He'd carried on courting her for a couple of years, and at one point, assumed he would marry her.

Until he got cold feet and left for London.

He wasn't stupid. He knew Mary was devastated. She'd thought the same about their future.

Before he'd left, he'd made it clear that he didn't know if, or when, he would be returning to Swansea. Morgan told her not to wait for him. He didn't know if Mary had been involved with anyone since, as he'd never asked her.  The sad thing was, he wasn't bothered if she had.

But he had a feeling he would if Ria had.

He sighed and swept his gaze back onto the road. He really shouldn't have been persuaded by his parents to see Mary again. It wasn't fair on her to dig something old back up.

What he needed was to think long and hard about his situation. Especially about what Ria would expect from him if their relationship progressed. Because, if truth be told, he wasn't sure if he'd eventually treat her the way he'd treated Mary.


After Morgan contacted the Police and sorted out his flat, the week in London ended up being very pleasant.

Mary, as usual, was quiet, unassuming, and relaxing to be around.  They'd enjoyed the touristy things and leisurely time in numerous restaurants.

To Morgan's surprise, Darren had been around most of the time, too, apart from a couple of evenings when he visited friends. Darren had been especially humorous and charming to Mary, particularly in the lulls of conversation when Morgan found his thoughts turn to Ria.

However, the week away had not solved all Morgan's dilemmas concerning Ria. He still had an overwhelming desire for her; time away hadn't dimmed that because he saw her every time he closed his eyes. He knew he would like to get to know her; but how long could he date her without trying to bed her? It would be difficult, but Morgan knew pushing her too quickly could push her away. He decided that if he stood a chance with her, he needed her to know that she wasn't a quick fling. Being a truthful person, he wouldn't promise her anything long term. But, only time would tell.

Glad that some of the weight on his shoulders felt eased, Morgan made the decision to talk to Ria, tomorrow.

## Chapter 7

The end of the week arrived painfully slow for Ria. All week, she'd anxiously waited for Morgan to appear because she wanted the opportunity to talk to him. But he never arrived.

As the week progressed, she felt more and more deflated. Even her anger with him at his assumption that she'd sleep with him subsided too.

"Are you listening to me?" Karen asked, watching Ria carefully.

"Um, yes." Ria realised she'd have to be more careful. She'd been distracted all week, and so far, Ria hadn't had to explain her mood to anyone.

"Good," Karen said, her eyes narrowing on Ria. "Are you feeling alright?"

Sally chirped in. "You do look a little pale."

"Yes, I'm alright. Really," said Ria. She tucked into her lunch in an attempt to stop Karen, or anyone else, ask any more questions.

Ria was aware that everyone knew about the fight at the Christmas party, she'd felt the stares and heard the whispers. However, unlike Karen, no one else had witnessed Morgan kissing her under the mistletoe. She knew Karen wouldn't gossip about her. Anyway, she had a feeling her friend would love the fact that everyone would be wondering why their normally placid boss, would punch out a guest of one of the workers. And, more importantly, why he hadn't come back to work.  Feeling downcast at her last thought, Ria struggled to swallow her food.

Karen nudged Sally, who almost dropped her sandwich, and nodded towards Ria. "Why don't we have a girlie night tonight?" Karen suggested. "It will be a laugh. I'll even get Mam to bake us some Welsh cakes or chocolate cakes, too."

"Yum," said Sally.

Ria didn't answer.

Trying to muster up Ria's enthusiasm, Karen continued. "Then, after we have stuffed and pampered ourselves, we can catch a film at the cinema? I've heard they are screening, *Around the World in Eighty Days*.  I think David Niven and Shirley MacLaine are staring in it."

"Hmmm…" Ria glanced up from her food and sighed. Even the thought of a film and cake left her deflated! All she wanted was to go home, curl up with a good book, not a romance, and hibernate.

When Ria saw the concerned look on her friend's faces, she realised she needed to sort herself out. This wasn't her.

"What do you think?" Karen prompted.

"Unless you have something else on, Ria?" Sally said, to give Ria a get out if she wanted one.

"No, I'm not doing anything."  Ria smiled. It would do her the world of good to talk to her friends.

*Perhaps we could talk about Morgan? They might be able to help.*

"Yes, I'd like that." She smiled, feeling some relief.

Keeping it to herself hadn't helped. During the dark hours in bed, Ria had replayed their two kisses over and over. She had enjoyed them both. They'd turned her bones to jelly.

But, that's what frightened her the most.

Ria had always assumed she would save herself for marriage. But, after her experience with Morgan, she could understand why women were tempted to take things further. Morgan had managed to unleash powerful feelings and urges within her, ones that she'd never experienced before. She felt her cheeks flush and hoped her friends didn't notice. Some of those urges were growing and spreading, and she didn't know what on earth she had to do to get rid of them.

"You're not off with that John boy then, Ria?" Marge interrupted Ria's thoughts. She'd obviously been eavesdropping on their conversation.

"No," she replied briskly, not wanting to open up that topic. It would only lead onto the Christmas fiasco.

Karen raised her eyebrows at Marge. "Private conversation, between friends." She motioned between the three of them.

Crossing her arms over her chest, Marge turned away. "Only being friendly," she mumbled.

Sally sniggered under her hand while Karen made a face.

"She likes to know everything that goes on," said Sally as she leant forward.

*That was one of the problems.* Ria gave her friends a shaky smile, trying to ignore the tight feeling in her chest.

*Who was she trying to kid?* Morgan wouldn't risk the gossip, especially now after she had cold feet over sleeping with him. Why on earth would he be interested in seeing her again?

Although innocent, Ria wasn't naïve. She knew a man like Morgan was used to sophisticated women. If they didn't give him what he wanted, he would move on.

But, if she did see him again, would she have the strength to say 'no' again? Did she want to end up like Sarah Davies, discarded and disgraced by a Templeton man? No, not really. But...

Unsettled, Ria knew her emotions were putting her at odds with all her previous moral codes and convictions. But, what would she do? That was, *if* Morgan was still interested?

Between mouthfuls of food, which were as unappealing as sandpaper, Ria looked at her friends. The pleading looks on their faces made her chuckle.

*Perhaps she needed some fun to get all her jumbled up emotions into check?*

She certainly needed her friends to help with some of her issues and put things back into perspective. "Yes, of course. Let's enjoy ourselves tonight."

~~~~~

"Oh, I'm stuffed!" Karen sighed contentedly. She placed the last piece of cake into her mouth.

"Chocolate cake and martinis. Bliss!" Ria agreed. She plumped up a pillow and put it against the wall. She relaxed back onto Karen's bed.

Sally stretched out on the rug placed on the floor. Her hand spanned her full belly. "I'm stuffed, too."

Ria glanced around Karen's bedroom and experienced the familiar feeling of warmth.

The three girls had known each other since they were little. And, though the bedroom's decoration had changed from ponies to flowers, it still contained memories of their childhoods together.

Ria felt a tingle. She loved this room. She loved her friends.

Sitting up, Ria knew now was her chance. She took a deep breath and hoped to gain some confidence.

When Karen looked over, Ria smiled at her. Karen was leant back on a chair, her feet on the bedspread.

Ria had a feeling Karen would be the one who would be able to help her get her head around the 'Morgan situation'.

For as long as Ria could recall, Karen always had a flock of boys after her in school. Now, it was men. Out of the three of them, Karen was the one with the most experience, so it was logical to ask for her advice.

Sally was an entirely different kettle of fish. She was beautiful, and should by rights, have loads of men buzzing around her. But, to everyone's surprise, Sally had never particularly seemed interested in the opposite sex. Although she had been on a smattering of date, Sally said she was waiting for 'the one' to realise he loved her and sweep her off her feet. No one knew who 'the one' was because she wouldn't even tell her friends.

"All we need now are the men!" Karen laughed.

Ria noticed the mischievous smile on Karen's lips. She knew her friend well enough to know what she was up to. She'd brought up the conversation of men so that she could quiz her about Morgan. R

"Or shall we just talk about them instead? It could be more fun?" Karen swivelled around to face Ria.

"So, Ria. Now you have a couple of drinks in you, would you like to let your friends in on your gossip?"

"What gossip?" Ria laughed.

"Don't give us that," Karen snorted. "What exactly happened when you kissed dreamy boss?"

Ria noticed Sally suddenly sit up. It was obviously the first time she had heard of it. "What?"

"That kiss under the mistletoe was steaaaamy!" Karen dragged out the last word.

Ria leant forward and crossed her legs. She was silently glad that she hadn't needed to broach the subject herself. "I don't know. I'm confused." She looked at her friend's wide eyes. "I fancy him, I mean who wouldn't?  He is so handsome."  She felt a blush rise, finding talking about it even difficult with her friends. "And that kiss. Well, I haven't experienced anything like *that* before."

"It's most probably because Morgan is a man, not a boy," said Karen. She looked thoughtfully at Ria, knowing she needed to be careful how she worded her response. After all, she wanted Ria to give Morgan a go. "He's in a different league to the guys around here. That's for sure. He's mature, so he might have loads of experience, but that doesn't mean he isn't a decent person. And he is handsome."

Ria gave her a shaky smile.

*He certainly was.*

But at the moment, Ria didn't know if that was going in his favour or not. Her forehead creased. "But, that's part of the problem, I think."

"How?" questioned Sally.

"Your Tom's handsome, and he's okay." Karen knew Ria loved her brother to bits, so assumed he would be a good example.

Ria gave Karen a playful tap on her leg. "You leave Tom out of this. Tom is half the problem."

"How?"

"Well, because of his looks, he's been out with most of the girls around here. He can go out with almost anyone he wants. But," Ria paused wanting to explain the best she could. "Tom never settles down with anyone. As far as I can see, he has his fun, and then gets rid of them."

Karen winced. Perhaps he wasn't a good choice to compare Morgan with? "He can have *his fun* with me anytime," Karen joked in an attempt to lighten the atmosphere.

"Yuk. I don't think I could handle you and my brother." Ria shook her head and laughed at the absurdity. "Anyway, I expect Morgan Templeton is after the same thing as Tom."

"What?" asked Sally.

Both Karen and Ria looked at each other and giggled.

"Oh, alright. I get it." Sally waved her hand at her friends.

"Don't tell me Morgan couldn't have *anyone* he set his eyes on. So, while I am flattered that he seems to like me, I am also scared stiff that I will just be a notch on his bedpost. It is something I don't want," Ria reasoned and then giggled. "I *think*."

Once they'd stopped laughing, Ria continued. "I *think* I want the long term thing. Marriage, kids, and everything." Ria cuddled the pillow in her arms a little closer.

"The way he was kissing you, he seems to more than like you." Karen narrowed her eyes in consideration. "Anyway, what's wrong with getting some experience *before* you get married?

"Karen," exclaimed Sally.

"What?" she replied. "I, for one, am sick and tired of the double standards. It's alright for a man to go out and sleep with anything that moves, but *so* wrong for the girl. Well, stuff that! I'm going to know exactly how to keep my husband happy in the bedroom.

Shocked at her friend's confession, Sally kept her opinion to herself and then giggled. It was so like Karen. Sally put her hand over her mouth, trying to stifle her giggles. "But, seriously. What about the gossips? Don't they bother you?"

"No, not really," Karen hesitated. "Besides, most people are hypocrites. I bet you half the people who marry should *not* be wearing white. At least, I'm honest... and young, and alive, and enjoying myself!" Karen looked at Ria. "Anyway, enough about me. What about you Ria? You wouldn't like to be a *notch*?"

"No... well, I never thought I would. But I was confused the other night." Ria ignored Karen when she raised her eyebrows towards Sally. She carried on, needing to tell them. "I know I might sound old-fashioned to you, but it's how I feel... I think." She picked at the corner of the pillow. "Oh, I don't know anymore, I'm so confused."

"Why were your confused the other night?" Sally said slowly.

"Do you mean the after the Christmas kiss?" Karen said.

Ria looked down and then back at her friends from under her lashes. They didn't know the next bit of her story. "After that fiasco in the Christmas party, I went down to the beach to cool off."

Both girls looked at each other, puzzled.

"You know... when you both took John home for me?"

"Yes..." replied Sally.

"I was so annoyed with the two of them. John, because he had too much to drink and was all over me. And Morgan because he had no right to hit John." She watched as her friends nodded their agreement. "Anyway, Morgan came to the beach."

"What! Did he follow you? You kept that quiet!" Sally's jaw almost hit the floor.

"No. I don't think he followed me. I think it must be a place where he goes to cool off. Like me."

"Convenient," mumbled Karen and then laughed. "Only joking." She put her head to the side. "Continue."

"Anyway, he asked me to *ask him* to kiss me – and I did!"

"Nooo!  Wow, how come you haven't mentioned this before tonight? How could you keep that secret?" Karen asked.

Ria blushed. "I don't know. I wanted to tell you both... but what could I say? The kiss was... was..."

"Toe-curling, blood curdling?" Karen filled in the blanks.

"Yes. It was breath-taking. I find it hard to describe. I was so caught up in the kiss that I think he could have undressed me there on the beach!"

Sally watched Ria wide-eyed, her mouth hidden under her hands.

"So what stopped you?" Karen asked seriously.

"Karen!" reprimanded Sally. She had never been kissed properly by a man, so sometimes she found

Karen too forward - even though she loved her, and her wicked ways.

"Me? Him? Oh, I don't know, I was all jumbled up. I'd never, ever felt like that before. But, the reality of it is that he only wanted to sleep with me. He invited me back to his house!"

"No," murmured Sally.

"Why didn't you go?" Karen questioned.

"When he asked me, I realised that I couldn't go through with it. But I know that if he kept kissing me, and not asked me home, I most probably wouldn't have hesitated! But, he gave me time to think. Look, it is not as though I think any worse of you Karen, but I realised that it was not what I want."

"Oh, thanks," Karen exaggerated her reply, not taking offence to her friend's words.

"The gossip that surrounds him and his brother sprung into my mind. And I really, *really* do not want to be a notch, however good looking he is."

"Oh, what did he say when you explained that to him?" asked Sally, finally removing her hands from her face.

"Well, I didn't in so many words. I just got angry because I was embarrassed. I thought that he might just see me as a young, inexperienced girl".

"Which you are," interjected Karen.

"Yes, well, I know... but I didn't want him to think I was inexperienced. But I didn't want him to believe I was easy either." Ria was struggling to explain her actions even now. "So I got angry and walked away. And now I am so embarrassed to see him again, but I also want to see him again. Oh girls, help me. I am so mixed-up."

Karen got off her chair and sat on the bed next to Ria. She draped her arm around her friend. "Now, I'm no expert," she winked at Sally, who giggled. "But, I see you have two choices. The first is: forget about him. If you don't feel comfortable with him wanting to go further, don't get into a situation that will allow it to happen - stay well away from him.

The second is: forget about the gossips, enjoy yourself, and see where the situation takes you. Don't let him force you into anything you don't want, though. Personally, from what I can tell, he's a decent person. Explain that you want to take things slower, and if he's prepared to do that, I believe he's a keeper."

Ria smiled with relief. "Thanks, girls. You don't know how important you both are to me. Come on, group hug."

They all jumped on the bed to hug each other.

## Chapter 8

Morgan rolled his shoulders, took a long deep breath, and sat back against his seat. He was back at the factory. The accounts lay in front of him, almost forgot in his thoughts.

He had arrived early, before anyone else. He tried to kid himself that he was early to catch up on his work, but as the accounts still lay hardly touched in front of him, he knew that was not the reason.

He wanted to see Ria.

Morgan grabbed his cold coffee and briefly wondered whether the extra caffeine would be good for his already wired system. He didn't care, all her wanted was to speak to Ria.

Now he had made up his mind about wanting to see her; he'd enough of waiting. When they spoke, he was going to apologise for his previous behaviour, and explain that he wanted to court her, not just sleep with her.

He took his final gulp of coffee and felt his anxiousness increase. It was nearly time for the workers to arrive.

A while later, Morgan heard the familiar factory noises. He got out of his seat and walked over to the mirrored wall. He watched as a steady stream of workers arrived. Each hung up their coats and put on their overalls and hats.

He continued to stand by the one-way window, hoping to catch sight of Ria, but all he saw was workers greeting each other and chatting. He couldn't hear what they were saying from his office, but the conversations looked animated this morning.

Quickly losing patience, Morgan searched the faces, wondering where Ria was. Something niggled him. The feeling worked its way through his system. He rolled his shoulders again, not knowing if it was the caffeine or just the agitation of waiting.

By the time the bell rang for the start of work, and the workers began to amble towards their stations, Morgan was concerned that Ria hadn't arrived.

Frustrated, but not knowing what he could do about it, Morgan sat back down on the leather seat and attacked the accounts.


Ria put her hand on her mother's and squeezed. She looked at her mother's tear-stained face. The despair etched on it suddenly made Megan seem so much older than her forty-five years. "Okay, Mam?"

Megan didn't reply.

Ria felt her emotions rise in her throat, choking her. She tried to suffocate them. She needed to be strong for her mother and siblings, not fall apart like she so desperately felt like doing.

It already seemed like a distant foggy memory, but Ria recalled what had happened just an hour ago.

She had just put her coat on, ready to leave for work when, Ivan, the foreman from the mines arrived, knocking on their door.  Ria instantly knew there was a problem because Ivan was out of breath and covered in the coal dust that all the miners showered off before leaving work.

She'd felt the blood drain out of her when Ivan informed her that there had been an explosion down the mine. Six miners were missing - her Dad and Michael were amongst them.

When Ivan left to go to inform the other families of the awful news, Ria turned towards the kitchen door and listened to her mother hum while she cleared the kitchen after breakfast.

Ria took a steadying breath, and even though she felt like collapsing into a ball and crying, she entered the kitchen, ready to tell her mother the awful news.

"Mam?" Ria prompted a response. "Anne said that Doris is up now. She saw her lights come on.  Anne will go and fetch her, and then we can go down to the mine together. To see if there is any news." She squeezed her mother's hand, concerned that she wasn't getting any reaction. "I know Tom is already there, but you might feel better if you were nearer. Doris will come and look after Johnny. Sam can go with us when he gets up. He doesn't need to go to school today..."

"Oh, I don't like to bother Doris, not after her husband..." Megan suddenly interrupted as tears filled her eyes.

Ria willed her tears away.

She vividly remembered when Doris's husband got trapped down the mine. The hours of waiting, the awful news that he had not survived, the months and years of grieving. Ria desperately hoped that her family wouldn't have to go through the same fate.

When Ria noticed Anne enter the kitchen, she nodded at her to indicate that she should go and fetch their neighbour. Ria felt a surge of pride when she noticed that Anne, too, tried to keep her tears in check. Their top priority was their mother.

Ria half watched as Anne slipped out, her attention back to her mother. She patted her hand, in what she hoped was a comforting gesture. Ria quietly sighed. Her mother wasn't aware of what was going on, she was in shock. "Don't worry, Mam. Doris will want to know that there had been an accident down the mine. I know Dad and Michael will be alright. They were on the same shift, so they'll look after each other." Ria hoped that by saying the words aloud they would come true.

Ria glanced up when she felt her mother shudder. She could see her attempt to pull herself together.

Ria helped her to stand, as she used the table for support.

"Yes, yes, let's go. I want to be there when your Dad and Michael walk out of that mine," Megan said. Neither her husband or child were dead, yet.

Morgan ran his fingers through his hair. He had solidly worked his way through the accounts for three hours. And it felt like it.

He'd been determined not to check if Ria had come into work. He kidded himself that this was work, and his personal life was separate. He laughed to himself.

*Who was he trying to kid?*

Morgan tried not to think of Ria, but it was useless. He found his mind wandering towards her whenever he had a spare second.

Morgan let out a short breath.

*How on earth could he still be thinking of her when looking at accountancy sheets?*

Standing, he went over to pour himself a fresh coffee. Not being able to help himself, he then wandered over to the window.

Looking over the factory floor, he soon realised Ria was not in. His eyes narrowed. Coming to think of it, the factory looked half empty. He was baffled.

Morgan turned towards the door when he heard a sharp knock. Something wasn't right, and he had a feeling in his gut that he was just about to find out.

Andrew Jones entered.

Morgan noticed how agitated he looked. "What's wrong? Why is the factory floor half empty?" Morgan questioned him immediately.

"Oh dear, oh dear…. Haven't you heard? I thought Helen, my secretary, would have been up to tell you. There was an accident at the mines. Six men are still missing… half the workers are up there." Jones snorted while he patted his stomach.

Morgan continued to watch him, a little stunned at the news.

Andrew Jones continued. "Everyone knows someone. That's the trouble sometimes with a small community. I've spent the morning trying to arrange cover, but if they are not already in work, they are down the mines waiting for word."

Morgan felt a tightening in his stomach.

*Didn't Andrew mention Ria had family working down the mines?*

The urge to go and find her was overwhelming. The need to protect and look after her, crushing. Fed up with fighting his feelings, Morgan placed his cup on his desk and strode to the door. "I'm going to the mines to see if there is anything the Templetons can do to help."

He left Andrew Jones mumbling to himself.

The area was crowded with people. Some pale with shock, some crying. In a close-knit mining community, whenever there was a crisis, everyone volunteered their services. People were huddled together. Some whispered, some too shocked to comment, but all of them aware that time was the enemy for the men trapped. The longer it was before news, the worse it usually was.

Morgan squinted against the low winter sun. It looked like the whole town was there. He was glad it wasn't raining, as usual, to make things worse for the waiting families. And, of course, for those in the mine.

Morgan found Ria instantly. Her family were bunched around a lady, whom Morgan assumed was their mother.

He took a deep breath, trying to control the urge to go over and hold Ria in comfort.

*He had no right.*

From afar, Morgan attempted to gauge how she was. Her skin looked pale against her fiery hair, but her emerald eyes looked alert as she gazed towards the office. They all knew that any news would come from that office.

He needed to go over to her, so he slowly made his way over, occasionally sidetracked by a worker who wanted a chat.

Ria noticed Morgan. Her belly did a flip.

*Was he coming over to her?*

She watched him take his time, talking to employees from the factory. From their smiles, she assumed he was offering comforting words.

Suddenly, a calmness came over her.

*He was making his way over to her.*

"Hello, Ria." Morgan nodded at her family. "I have just heard the news and have come to see if there is anything the Templetons can do to help you and the other families?"

Ria noticed the concern lacing his voice and felt awful that, for a moment, he'd made her forget what was happening around her.

She gave him a wavering smile and averted her eyes. "Mam, Tom, Anne, Sam. This is Mr Templeton from the factory." Ria didn't fail to detect the concerned look he had in his eyes as he checked her face before he turned towards her mother and siblings.

"Please, call me Morgan." He held out his hand in greeting. "I am so sorry to hear about the explosion. Is there any more news?"

Tom replied for his mother, absentmindedly running his hand up and down her back. "No, they have moved in the machines and are trying to drain away the water. Hopefully, there isn't…" he glanced at his mother and changed what he was going to say. "They haven't made contact yet with any of the six down there."

Ria put her arm around her mother's waist when she noticed the tremble on her mother's lips.

Morgan put his hands in his pockets. He felt useless. He was desperate to give Ria some comfort, too. Needing some distance before he gave into his urges and grabbed her, he excused himself from their company.

He turned and went to see if there was anything he could do. To see if his family name would help. He smiled dolefully. Usually, he would never use his family's standing to his advantage, but this was one time he counted it as a blessing.

As he walked away, Morgan recognised the foreman, Bill Thomas. He was a good friend of his father. He stopped when he noticed Bill walk towards him.

"Oh, Morgan. Am I glad to see you," said Bill, out of puff. "We're having difficulty trying to keep the lines of communication open between everyone. Would you be able to help us out?" He raised his large eyebrows in question. "I know you're busy, but you know most of the people here by name, and so time will be spared."

Morgan noticed that Bill's face was etched with lines of worry and stress.

"Martin Cole is doing the job now, but he's new to the village, so he doesn't know people's names." Bill shook his head. "It's not right shouting out names."

"Of course," Morgan interrupted. "Anything I can do to help, Bill." Morgan was relieved that he wouldn't be useless.

"Come with me."

Morgan followed Bill into the office.

As soon as they entered the office, Bill asked, "Has anything developed? Have you made any contact with those inside?"

A man standing by the phone shook his head.

Bill turned to Morgan. "All we know so far is that six men are trapped down there." He handed Morgan a clipboard with a list of names. "These are the records of the families involved." Bill pointed out of the window. "We have set up a tent for them, with refreshments. Not that I can imagine they want any. Anyway, would you go out and get them in away from all the other onlookers? I am sure they don't want people crowding around them when they are waiting for news. Good or bad." Bill lowered his head in contemplation.

"Consider it done, Bill," replied Morgan.

"Okay, I'll catch you later."

When Bill left, Morgan glanced down at the names on the list. Ria's Dad and brother's names caught his attention.

Once the affected families were housed as comfortably as possible under the circumstances, Morgan made his way back to the office for an update.

Men, some covered in soot, gathered around the large table that dominated the office. Plans were spread out over it.

"Is this the latest diagram of the mines?"

Bill nodded.

The man, who was in charge of the rescue mission, carried on. "I want to know the exact location of the explosion, and where you would expect the men to be located."

Bill pointed to an area on the map. "From what we can determine, the explosion was in this area."

"Are there any shafts, such as ventilation, that aren't shown on these maps?"

Morgan stood back while the men chatted among themselves, going over different scenarios.

Although he tried not to listen, from what Morgan could make out, the best scenario was that the miners were behind a wall of rock and coal. The worst - Morgan did not even want to listen to that. What he did know was if they were to have *that* outcome, it would affect the whole community. He didn't even want to think about the effect it would have on Ria and her family.

Morgan tried to put thoughts of Ria on the backburner. This wasn't the time. Now was a time for clear thinking, not emotions. He sipped his cold tea.

Over time, the noise of ringing telephones increased, and more people arrived. Families and friends came offering support, and the media turned up. The silent concentration inside the office was considerably juxtaposed with the going-ons outside the room.

Minutes turned into hours, and the anxiety levels, both inside and outside the office, rose as time slipped away.

Ria felt the burden of uselessness. It did not matter how many cups of tea she told her mother to drink, or food that she tried to tempt her with, the empty look in her mother's eyes made her feel useless.

The people around her were given sandwiches and refreshments, but Ria noticed that most of it stayed drying and curling on their plates.

Ria glanced up when she felt Morgan enter the room. She noticed him search her out. She tensed, not knowing if she wanted to hear any news or not.

When he made eye contact, he shook his head.

Ria left out a breath. She was relieved there wasn't any bad news, but she felt the keen disappointment squeeze her belly that there wasn't good news. She daren't think of her father and brother down in the dark, each minute must feel like forever for them.

Ria continued to watch Morgan as he poured a couple of cups of coffee. When he turned and walked towards them, she noticed dark circles under his eyes. A surge of tenderness fluttered through her. Ria was very aware that Morgan didn't have any family or friends down the mine, but it seemed as though the tension and waiting was taking its toll on him, too.

What Ria didn't know was that some of the shadows were due to the sleepless nights he had spent, thinking of her.

As Morgan started to walk over with the coffees, he spotted the Rescue Supervisor stride into the office. Quickly he turned and placed the coffees on the nearest table. He shot an apologetic smile at Ria and hurried back into the office.

Some of the waiting families had seen the Supervisor, too. Some hadn't failed to notice that he was less tense than before. Murmurs increased, as a ripple of hope went around the families.

Ria instinctively huddled nearer to her mother. She was afraid to hope for good news, although silently she longed for it. Squeezing her eyes tight, Ria tried to control her wayward heart. She prayed that Morgan would come back through the door with the good news.

"They're alive! They're alive!"

Ria's head whipped around towards the commotion. She saw Morgan and a coal-covered man enter the refreshment area.

Families surged forward, desperate to find out more details.

"Are they out?"

"Are they all alive?"

"Are they hurt?"

People shouted from every direction. Relief and desperation made them demand answers.

Morgan needed to take charge of the situation. He waved his arms in the air to quieten the crowd down.

The need to know what Morgan was going to say made the crowd self-regulate themselves.

When they settled, Morgan addressed them. "Please, I know it is difficult, but please be patient. We will give you all the information we have now, and then John can answer any questions after." He nodded towards John. "The rescue team have just made contact with the men through an air shaft. From what we can gather, miraculously no one is hurt."

He waited until the increase in noise settled again.

"From what we can gather, there are some minor cuts and bruises, which will be dealt with when they get them out. The ambulance crew are waiting." He put his hands up again, as the talking increased. "Remember, we still need to get them out, but everything looks stable down there."

A cheer went around the room. The oppressive atmosphere that once filled the room, lifted. People started to crowd around John with more questions.

Morgan, having completed his duty for Bill and the families, sidestepped the crowd.

*Where is she?*

Morgan made his way through the masses to the corner where Ria stood apart from the crowd. His heart tightened as he noticed tears fall down her cheeks.

Through blurred eyes, she smiled at Morgan when he headed over to her. An enormous surge of emotions hit her. Relief and happiness mainly.

"Hi," he said.

Unable to distinguish one emotion from another, Ria threw herself at Morgan. She needed to hug him. As she nestled into his broad chest, Ria felt his arms tighten around her.

Morgan bent and pressed his cheek against the crown of her head. It felt so good.

Ria breathed in deeply. It felt like it was the first time she could breathe properly. Ria felt safe cradled in his arms. She sighed, wishing she'd had the courage to do this a couple of hours before.

All the previous tension of the day, and the frustration of not being able to touch Ria, flowed right out of Morgan. He resisted the urge to kiss the top of her head, but he breathed in her scent.

It felt so right, cradling her in his arms. She was the perfect fit.

Tears fell freely from Megan's eyes. Both her husband and son were safe! After hugging Tom, Alice, and Sam, she looked for Ria.

Then she found her. In an embrace with Mr Templeton.

A smile tickled one side of her mouth. Perhaps it was time to give her daughter some space? Turning away, Megan carried on hugging all around her.

After a couple of minutes of silence, Morgan spoke. "They will be alright now, Ria. They're alright." He couldn't help it, he gently kissed the top of her hair. "They will get them out, and then they will have to go to the hospital to get checked out." He used on hand to stroke his fingers through her hair, using the other one to keep her close.

Ria breathed in deeply, comforted by his words. She closed her eyes, contented.

Suddenly, they sprung open. Heat rose in her cheeks as reality slammed into her. Mortified, Ria realised she had jumped into his arms. She felt uncomfortable. Ria stepped out of his embrace and lowered her gaze towards the floor. She didn't want him to see the blush of embarrassment growing on her face. "Thank you for your help, Mr Templeton," she managed to mumble.

"Uh?" He pushed his hand through his hair.

*What just happened? How did she change so fast? And why was she back to calling him Mr Templeton.* Morgan glanced around to see what had affected her. Everyone in the room were too busy hugging and chatting to notice them. His gaze focused back on to her.

Digging deep for courage, Ria looked up at his face. She could see he looked confused. "Morgan, I'm sorry. Thank you for your help today, I am sure everyone has appreciated everything you have done."

Morgan inwardly sighed. She'd backed off. He'd noticed the blush on her cheeks and correctly assumed Ria had become embarrassed that she hugged him. But, he enjoyed having her in his arms and certainly didn't want her to feel uncomfortable. "Ria," he said with a sigh. "Come with me."

Morgan gently grabbed her elbow, then steered her towards the chairs that someone had thoughtfully provided for the waiting families. When she sat, he walked over to the refreshment area.

After he had poured two coffees, he returned, handing her one. "It looks a bit like mud, but at least it's warm."

Ria reached out to take it. She gave him a shaky smile before taking a sip.

"Stay here and recover a bit, while your mum and brother get things sorted out with the medics." He nodded to them while taking a sip of his awful coffee. Turning back he looked at her over the rim. "You don't seem in any fit state at the moment."

Ria shrugged, suddenly too tired to respond. She knew she'd look a mess, this morning had taken it out of her. She secretly hoped she didn't look too bad in front of Morgan!

Sitting silently, Ria kept the coffee firmly wrapped in her hands. It acted as some sort of barrier. What she wanted was to be back in his arms, and to tell him that his presence had made the experience so much easier to deal with. But, she couldn't. The words wouldn't form. Besides, she'd only make a fool of herself. He was the boss and he'd been just as supportive with everyone else.

*Hadn't he?*

She looked down at her lukewarm coffee.

Morgan noticed her fingers wrapped tightly around her cup. She was still tense. He wanted her to relax, especially now that her family was alright. She'd had enough stress for one day.

Not entirely sure of what to do, he hoped that it wasn't him that she was tense with.

*Perhaps she wanted him to go?*

He didn't want to.

Before he thought too much about it, he blurted out, "Victoria, now that your family are safe, would you like to come out with me on the weekend? A sort of celebration that everyone is fine?" He held his breath in anticipation, desperate for her to say *yes*.

Ria was momentarily shocked. That was the last thing she'd expected him to say. She was about to stutter out 'yes' when she caught a movement in the corner of her eye.

It was Marge, from the factory.

Marge was crying and squeezing her husband, the first man to be rescued unhurt from the mine.

Out of the blue, Ria's lip curled in amusement. The way Marge hugged him, she was sure he would need the hospital for broken ribs!

As she tore her gaze away, she remembered Marge's words of warning about the Templeton men. Panic overrode her feelings for Morgan. "I can't go out with you. People will talk. You're the factory owner's son. It just isn't right," she blurted out.

Morgan watched the myriad of emotions rush across her face. At first, when she'd smiled, he thought she was going to say 'yes'. Morgan glanced at the spot Ria had been looking at, to pinpoint her discomfort. He only spotted Marge from the factory but didn't know why she would be a problem.

He turned back to Ria.

*Did it matter to her what people thought?*

It never had to him, but perhaps, by having money, he had unconsciously bypassed that problem.

*What did she mean by 'right'?*

He didn't see spending time together as wrong. Not wanting her to get off that easily, he took a step towards her and bent down, eye level.

Morgan put a finger under her chin and gently raised it. "I would love to spend time with you, Ria." He waited until she looked at him properly. "Do you fancy coming to the Mumbles with me on Saturday, and then perhaps the Museum? Would that be all right for you?"

Ria broke eye contact and her gaze flittered around the room. She thought about her work colleagues and the gossip, but then seeing happy people, it made her think about today's events.

A good lesson on how short life could be.

Ria returned her gaze to his. The look in his eyes overrode her nervousness. "Yes, yes, thank you. I would love to go out with you on Saturday."

"Great," a broad smile appeared on his face.

## Chapter 9

When Ria woke up on Saturday, she was a bundle of excitement and nerves

Trying to concentrate on her makeup, she noticed her intense excitement made her skin glow. She smiled.

*What was it going to be like spending the day with him?*

She applied some lipstick she borrowed off Karen.

*Would he kiss her?*

She giggled nervously as butterflies flitted through her stomach. She shook her head. She'd have to get in control. Otherwise, it would be embarrassing if she acted like a giggly schoolgirl!

Once she'd calmed, Ria stared at her reflection. She wondered what he saw in her. Suddenly she stiffened.

*What happened if he was only taking her out because he had felt sorry for her at the mines? Don't be silly.*

She knew it wouldn't do her any good to think like that, so she pulled herself together again. As she brushed her hair, Ria decided that she was going to stop analysing the situation and then hopefully, enjoy their day.

When Ria finished and felt more settled, she made her way down the stairs into the kitchen.

She opened the door. Her parents were already having breakfast.

Evan, recovered from his ordeal down the mine, looked at her over his morning paper. "You're up early, my lass." He noticed that she had her best clothes on and makeup. Not usual for a regular Saturday. "Going somewhere?"

"Mr Templeton, my boss, is taking me to the Mumbles and the Museum today." She sent a fleeting glance towards her father. "You met the other day, Mam, at the mines."

"Yes, I did. Nice gentleman," Megan said raising her eyebrows at Evan. A silent warning not to say too much.

Evan's brow puckered while he digested the information.

"Yes, he is," said Ria trying to gauge her father's mood.

Evan sighed. His little girl was not so little anymore. But, regardless, he felt uneasy that his daughter was going out with her boss's son who was a grown man. "What do you know about him?"

"Evan," Megan tutted.

"Um," Ria tried to think of something other than she fancied him!

His wife's reprimand had him thinking. Regardless of whether he'd seen too many relationships fail because they didn't come from the same background, did he have any right to meddle in her life? She was a working woman after all. He glanced at Megan, who was giving him 'the look'.

Evan sighed again. Young love would never listen to reason. They always thought they knew better than their parents. "Just be careful, my girl. He seemed pleasant enough, but he is much older than you, and he is the factory owner's son."

"Come on now, Evan. Mr Templeton is only taking her out for the day. Let her have some fun. After the accident with you and Michael, and helping me with Johnny, she deserves some time off," Megan playfully scolded him.

A smile beamed on Ria's face. "Thanks, Mam, Dad. I will be back for tea. Love you!"

They both watched, each filled with different worries and concerns, as their daughter left the kitchen.


Ria loved their trip to the Mumbles on the train, even though the ride had been bumpy at times. Embarrassingly, she'd fallen off her chair into Morgan a number of times. Every time she'd done it, she pretended to look out of the windows because she could feel the colour rise in her cheeks.

While they were travelling, Morgan explained that the company that owned the Mumbles train wanted to sell it off. So, as a result, they weren't repairing the track. Hence the bumps.

Ria hated the idea of it being sold. She'd always loved going to the Mumbles, and didn't want the train to be scrapped. "That's such a shame. I remembered celebrating its 150th anniversary a couple of years ago. All of Swansea's schoolchildren had the day off and we all dressed in period costumes." She smiled. "It was even filmed for the television."

"Times change," Morgan tried to reason. But, he too, didn't like the idea any more than her. "It's a shame, though. It even survived the bombings during the war."

"I know," she said looking out of the window at the passing beach. Hopefully, it was just hearsay.

When they arrive back in town, they made their way to the museum. When they reached it, Morgan placed his hand on the small of her back to help direct her up the Museum steps.

Ria felt the warm glow of the contact. She felt hyper-aware of him, but she was becoming more comfortable in his company.

Throughout the day, Morgan had been great company. He'd surprised her too by being so knowledgeable about the things around Swansea.

Morgan pulled her out of her thoughts when he leant forward and whispered in her ear. She had to stop herself flinching as his hot breath gently tickled her earlobe. It was nice.

"Do you realise that once, these Museum steps, were where the *ladies of the night* frequented?"

"No," Ria giggled.

"They used to wait for the returning sailors, the *Cape Horners,* who had pockets full of wages. The women wanted to snag them before they returned to their families."

Ria turned slightly. Not too much as his lips were still near to her ear. It would be too tempting to kiss them. "Who were the *Cape Horners*?" Ria knew because she had been taught about them in school, but she liked listening to him.

He straightened back up and Ria keenly felt the lack of intimacy.

"They were the crew of the sailing ships, called barques. They were involved in the copper trade, delivering copper ore from around the world to the copper smelting areas of Swansea." He nodded towards the old dock area. "They embarked from Swansea's new North and South Docks, often travelling up to 8,000 miles on voyages. They lasted up to several months, even up to a year."

"That's a long time to be at sea."

Morgan nodded. "Yes. They travelled all over the world to get the ore. To Central and South America, the East Indies, Calcutta, and later to Spain, South Africa, Cuba, Newfoundland, Chile, Venezuela, and even Australia."

Morgan took Ria's hand and continued his story. "The long, arduous voyages often went around South America via Cape Horn. That was before the Panama Canal was made." He resisted the urge to play with her fingers. "They went to Chile and then back. But Cape Horn was notorious for its winds, so the men could sail for days and then be pushed back again by the wind."

"Great," she said, trying to concentrate on what he was saying, not doing.

"Remember, they didn't have engines to help them, only their sails. Eventually, the sailors became known as the Cape Horners. It's a sign of a good sailor."

Morgan's gaze strayed onto their interlocked hands.

Ria's heart beat and breathing increased. It was too difficult to concentrate, so she carefully removed her hand.

Morgan didn't comment. He put his hands in his pockets.

"Imagine living without your family for months at a time. I couldn't imagine leaving mine for any length of time." Ria glanced towards the direction of the docks. She sighed. "I expect a lot of lives, and cargo must have been lost. Disease, bad weather and accidents." Ria's forehead creased while she thought of all those poor sailors - lost, leaving their loved ones alone. It was such a hard life.

Morgan found her compassion endearing. "Yes, many men didn't survive. They were buried at sea, or in a place called Santiago. Santiago became known as the 'Swansea Graveyard'. It was a harsh time." Suddenly, he wanted to shake off the deflated mood. "Come on. Let's go in."

Ria didn't want to go in yet. They were alone on the steps and she didn't wish to enter the crowded museum yet. She continued to talk to prolong their departure. "What did they want the copper ore for, to travel all that way?" From what he'd said so far, Ria assumed he listened a lot more in his History lessons than her!

"They needed copper. It's an easily workable metal used for things like cooking and industrial vessels. Even the Royal Navy used it, for things such as nails and sheathing for the boats. It stopped the wooden-hulled ships being attacked by wood-boring worms. The use of copper became worldwide."

Morgan noticed Ria shiver when a fresh breeze blew past them. "Come on. Let's get in out of the cold. Perhaps I can take you to the Copperworks tomorrow?" He smiled at her. "Just to finish off your education, of course?"

Ria smiled at him.

*I can't believe I've already asked her out!*

Before Morgan had come today, he'd promised himself not to rush her.

*Great job, so far!*

He reached out for her hand. This time, he was glad she didn't pull it away. "We'll talk about that later." After spending the morning with her, Morgan knew that he wanted to see her again. "Let's go," he said as they started up the rest of the steps.


As Ria got into bed, she had to stop herself from humming. Even getting changed in the cold bedroom hadn't seemed so bad.

Glancing at Anne, she could see she was already fast asleep.

*Well, she was home late.*

She hadn't wanted the day to end!

Morgan had been excellent company. He was always conscious of her, making sure she was comfortable and happy. Every time he touched her or held her hand, Ria felt her pulse quicken. It was even racing now, just thinking about him.

Carefully, not to disturb Anne, Ria pulled the blankets over her. She laid back and looked at the ceiling rose. She sighed contentedly. She knew it would be ages before her mind or body would allow her to sleep.

As she snuggled down into her feather pillow, she continued to recall the day.

They'd had lunch at a little restaurant down the Mumbles. She'd also had a glass of wine that had made her feel tipsy. She'd never had wine with lunch before. It seemed so decadent!

Many times during the day she thought he was going to kiss her.

But he didn't!

He held her hand and touched her, but nothing more. When they'd arrived at her home, she'd felt disappointed. After their kiss on the beach, she had expected him to at least try. She'd even begun to think he was taking her out because he felt sorry for her at the time of the mining accident, again.

Ria crumpled the bedding up to her mouth to stop her erupting giggle. She might wake Anne. That all changed when he had walked her to her door.

*What a kiss.*

She sighed and smiled. Not that it mattered now, but unfortunately, the kiss had been cut short. It ended abruptly when the porch light had gone on. The light had nearly blinded the two of them.

Ria knew it was her father. He'd known *exactly* when to switch that outdoor light on. She laughed and snuggled further down, ready to let sleep take over. She decided that she would enjoy dreaming of Morgan tonight.

The winter sun that streamed through the bedroom window, woke Ria up early.

Once up and ready, Ria walked into the kitchen, humming as she went. She poured herself a coffee and, as customary, gave her mother and father a morning kiss.

As usual, Evan already sat by the pine table, a bowl of porridge, and cup of tea in front of him.

Her mother was scrubbing the porridge bowl in the sink before it stuck to the sides and became almost impossible to remove.

The rest of the house was quiet. Everyone was enjoying a weekend lie in, and no doubt, her older brothers would be nursing sore heads from a night at the Red Lion.

"You're up early on a Sunday," Evan said as he eyed his daughter suspiciously.

"Hmm."

He decided to take a different approach. "Off to Church with your Mam, are you, lass?" Evan asked, long ago knowing that Ria had outgrown Sunday School.

"No, I don't go anymore," Ria said.

Evan glanced at Megan who had that 'what are you up to?' look on her face.

He appreciated that these days the 'youngsters' only seemed to go to Church on special occasions. His wife, however, went with Doris every Sunday. They'd be making their way in about an hour. As he never went anymore, he couldn't blame the younger generation for not going.

To be honest, he'd always felt uneasy with, what he thought were, the constraints of the Church. Once his parents stopped having a say in his choices, he realised that religion wasn't for him. Besides, he was sure his wife did enough praying for him and his sins!

Ria gave her father a smile, fully aware that he was digging for information. "Morgan is taking me to the Copper Works today. We arranged it last night."

"Oh, that's what you were doing outside the door last night? Good job I put the light on for you then," he said with a laugh.

"Dad," Ria said feeling a blush rise.

Megan rolled her eyes at her husband. She could still remember *their* discussions.

On her parent's doorstep.

The Funny thing was, last night she'd wondered why he had suddenly got up during the News and put on the porch light. Now she knew what he had been up to. He knew *exactly* what would have been going on outside. Although it felt like a long time ago, they'd been young once.

Megan turned back towards the dishes and laughed.

*Perhaps a couple of extra prayers would be called for in Church today?*

~~~~

Morgan fashioned a mock bow. "Welcome to the White Rock Copper Works, Madam."

Ria giggled.

Standing back up, Morgan took her hand and gave it a kiss. He swept his other arm out, indicating for her to look at their surroundings. "Did you know that Swansea was called *Copperopolis* in the 18th and 19th centuries?"

Ria ran her fingers over the 1737 date plaque, embedded in stone. "Yes, I remember the Museum stated that 90% of all copper smelting in Britain in 18...?"

"1820," Morgan supplied her with the answer.

"...were based within 20 miles of the city," she supplied the rest quickly.

"Well done," Morgan said in his best 'teacher' voice. "You're a good student."

Happy and relaxed with the playful, teasing tone, he grabbed her close and encircled her with his arms.

"Morgan," she giggled, tapping his arm lightly.

He pulled her closer. He'd been eager to hold her in his arms yesterday, but he'd had decided to take it slow, not to frighten her off again. Morgan doubted Ria would ever appreciate how hard it had been for him to keep a distance.

To be honest, before the date, he had even vowed he wasn't going to kiss her. Luckily, he'd broken that promise. When he walked her to her parents' door, and she turned to say goodbye, his stomach had somersaulted. Breathtakingly beautiful, he just had to kiss her lips. He had no wish to control his desire any longer.

Morgan smiled about it now, although last night he had sworn under his breath. What effectively kerbed his desire for her was the bright light that had been turned on.

*What an excellent deterrent that had been. He would have to remember that trick when he became a father!*

But, thankfully, her father wasn't around now. So, he bent his head towards her ear. "What a good student you are. Let's see what else you can be taught...," he whispered.

Trembles of anticipation ran through Ria when she felt his breath on her lips. She felt his warm hands cup the back of her neck, and his mouth slowly descended to make contact with hers. Excitement swirled inside her, as her blood started to pound in her ears.

As his lips made a thorough exploration of hers, a moan parted her sweet lips for him. It was all the invitation he needed to explore her depths.

Wanting to get closer, Ria moved her arm up and pulled his head closer. She entwined her fingers in his thick, dark hair, keeping him exactly where she wanted.

As their tongues entwined, the need to be close was overwhelming for them both.

Removing one of his hands from around her neck, he used it to run up and down her spine, moulding her flat against his hard body.

As surges of pleasure claimed her body, it made Ria hot, unbearably so. Ria's clothes became an unwanted barrier.

Wrapped up in each other, physically and mentally, they both forgot where they were. A tip-tap of shoes, and a small, polite cough, nearly didn't cut through their haze of desire.

Morgan's body tensed at the intrusion he was vaguely aware of. Then reality hit. He sighed heavily before he removed his mouth from her warm lips. "Good job we are in a public place," he muttered quietly to Ria, his forehead resting on hers. When he heard another cough, he glanced up and gave the intruding woman a quick nod.

She scowled at them before turning on her heels and walking away.

"Oops," giggled Ria, embarrassed.

Morgan shrugged, unconcerned. Unable to totally break away from Ria, he fingered a strand of her hair. He brought it to his nose to smell, watching her. He was delighted she was still riding on her emotions. Her green eyes, half closed.

Flicking his gaze away, Morgan noticed another two women with their children come into view. He knew Ria was unaware of them.

They stopped and stared. It was as though they hadn't seen anyone hugging before. One of them grabbed their child's hand.

Not wanting to let Ria go, Morgan looked over Ria's shoulder at them and raised his eyebrows in question. He noticed their gazes sweep them up and down, returning to his arms around Ria. Morgan didn't care. He ignored their offended looks, keeping his arms firmly around her. He expressed amusement when in unison, the women huffed, turned and left.

"What was that?" Ria tried to turn in his arms.

"Nothing. Just a couple of women." Morgan looked down onto Ria's upturned face. He wanted to kiss her again, but more people had started to mill around, so he made conversation instead. "Do you know how appropriate your hair is here?"

"What do you mean?" Ria's brow creased.

Morgan couldn't help giving the furrow a little peck. "The beautiful copper colour?"

Ria giggled. "Funny."

"I mean it. It's such a beautiful colour."

"I've always hated it. It's been like a beacon for my brothers to pull it." She scowled.

Morgan laughed. "Well, hopefully, they are passed that now." He kissed the tip of her nose. "You should love it." As his gaze landed on her lips, the urge to kiss it was overpowering. However, another person passed them.

Finally, Morgan let out a breath of defeat. He let her go and stepped back to put a short distance between them. Besides, the next person could know them, and Ria would have to deal with gossip. Not that it bothered him, but Swansea could be a small place at times.

Grabbed for her hand, they carried on walking alongside the old furnaces. They were out of use now, but they once would have manufactured copper pans and pots to be distributed over Europe.

Hoping to find a quiet spot for them to be alone, they strolled along as he carried on telling her about the Copper Works. "The early copper and brass smelting industries moved to Swansea because of the coalfields. Smelting relied on vast amounts of coal, so it made sense to build the factories near the coal fields. And then import the copper from mining areas such as Devon and Cornwall.

The River Tawe could carry ships up to the smelting works, along the river side. The returning cargo of coal, went to the West Country, and was used to fuel steam engines pumping water out of the copper mines..."

Morgan scanned the area and realised that they were on their own again. He turned to her and put his arms back around her waist. It felt good.

Ria smiled up at him. "And?" she teased a smile playing on her lips.

Morgan bent to nibble her ear before he carried on. "During the Industrial Revolution, copper and brass were in such demand that two more copper smelters were built by 1780."

Ria giggled. His nibbles and warm breath were causing havoc with her system. "Stop," she laughed. "I can't concentrate."

"Oh, can't you? And I was going to test you later on," he teased. "Perhaps I can think up some form of punishment for wrong answers?" He raised his eyebrows in jest when she playfully swiped his chest.

"Continue," she said.

"Copper was being used for coins, fire-boxes, electrical transmission wire, and even candlesticks by then.

Unfortunately, like most industries, apart from the bosses benefiting, life was not so good for the people living in Swansea."

"Surprise, surprise," Ria murmured.

"Work-related accidents. Diseases from living and working so closely together. Illness from the work environment." He looked down and noticed her grave face. He decided to lighten the conversation. "To compensate, the bosses, however, built houses and churches for the workers." He started to punctuate each word with a kiss. "They even built… Welsh speaking… chapels on a …unprecedented scale." Each feather like kiss was making it harder for him to talk.

"I know, like the house that I live in?"

"Yes," he mumbled before he kissed his way down her jaw to her neck, where her pulse was beating frantically.

"But the communities had to live with the sulphur smoke produced by the Works. It produced acid rain that affected them and the farmlands." Morgan's last sentence was almost a whisper, as his attention was solely on Ria.

Her voice broke the spell. "Which is why the *rich* people moved over to the West side of the river, to get away from the smog and left the workers on the East. In the smog?"

Morgan felt Ria stiffen and try to pull away. He didn't let her.

"It must be nice to be able to buy your way out of life's problems." Ria reflected, bitterness lacing her voice.

Morgan was frustrated. Ria apparently felt that wealthy people were somehow better because they happened to be born into money. He sighed, and loosened his arms to circle her in a light grip. It gave him a better angle of her face. "Yes, to some extent. But, remember the rich did give back into the communities."

Ria's nose crinkled.

"Remember, when I was kissing your neck, I was talking about houses and chapels being built for the communities?"

Ria saw a smile playing at the corners of his mouth.

"Or were you too distracted by something?"

She giggled, but swiftly averted her eyes when she felt a blush rise up her cheeks. She quietly reprimanded herself.

*Why could she kiss him so freely one minute, and then be embarrassed by the thoughts of her actions, the next?*

Morgan thought the sudden attack of shyness very endearing. He didn't comment. He didn't want to make her more uncomfortable. "Take John Vivian for instance. In its day, his works were one of the most up-to-date industrial enterprises in the whole of Europe.

"Vivian & Sons were the largest exporters of copper in the UK. The Vivians built an area for their employees called *Vivianstown* or *Trevivian*. We know it as the *Hafod* today.

"They built a school, a church, and the housing the workers lived in. That wouldn't have happened without the money of the Vivians." Morgan lifted her chin with his finger. "People with money aren't all bad you know?" He hoped she listened to his words because he didn't want his wealth to become an issue between them. "Eventually, copper ore were smelted in their country of origin, and most of the copper industries around Swansea stopped in the 1920s."

"Doesn't the *Hafod and Morfa Copperworks* still deal with copper, though?" questioned Ria.

"Yes, but just secondary copper processing." He took in a breath. "And who's to say how long that's going to continue?"

Ria grew pensive. "I suppose it is the same for mining. Dad is always going on about people changing from coal fires to central heating. Perhaps the need for coal will disappear and Michael and Dad will be out of a job?"

With his feeling growing for Ria, he was suddenly uncomfortable that life for Ria and her family wasn't as straight forward as his. Morgan knew he had problems with family expectations at times. But, he wasn't naïve not to know that being born into money got rid of a lot of problems other people faced - paying bills, keeping warm, and even paying for medicines. Being born into money had its benefits.

Surprised at the protective feeling for her and her family, which knotted deep in his stomach, he grabbed her hand. He'd suddenly had enough of the copper works. "Come on, let's get you home.

"Will you promise to come to the cinema with me on Wednesday? They are showing the new film with Charlton Heston, Yule Brynner and Anne Baxter. It is called *The Ten Commandments*."

Ria smiled at him. "Yes, I would love to, but..." she paused, a concerned look suddenly marring her cold, flushed face. "I still don't want anyone to know about us at work, if that is all right? I just wouldn't feel comfortable if anyone knew that we were seeing each other." She smiled reticently. "I don't think I could manage all the gossip Marge would create."

Morgan appreciated what she meant. "Fine, if that is what you want." He kissed her on the tip of her chilly nose. "Hey, does that mean we have to hide in one of the dark corners of the stockroom then?"

She laughed and gently batted his arm.

"Because you know I can't keep my hands off you." He continued to chat and tease her while escorting her back to his car.

After entering the foyer of the cinema, Morgan and Ria walked over the heavily patterned Axminster carpet, which was immaculately clean and still smelled of 'new' carpet, towards the gold painted Pay Kiosk. The lady inside was dressed in a hat and matching uniform. Currently, she stared jadedly at a couple who were trying to enter an 'A' movie.

Ria watched as the woman scowled at the obviously young pair, before she threw a couple of tickets at them, waving them away.

"Two for the balcony, please," Morgan asked the same weary lady inside the kiosk.

Ria smiled to herself when she noticed the kiosk lady suddenly sit up straighter. She gave Morgan her best smile, but Morgan seemed totally oblivious.

While the woman, whose nametag said 'June', continued to sort out their tickets, Ria became excited. She had never sat in the balcony seats before. They were the best seats, and therefore, expensive.

"Hurry now, you two. The lights are just about to dim, and you don't want any tuts from the audience already seated, do you?" Realising that Morgan was treating his girlfriend, she added. "You might just have time to grab an ice cream from the usherette."

They watched *The Ten Commandments.* It was a long film, but Ria hadn't found it boring. How could she when Morgan sneaked a kiss in whenever he could.

Morgan enjoyed Ria pretending to watch the film. When he managed to distract her with his kisses, he liked the way she would playfully swat him, but secretly smile.

At the end of the film, they stood for the National Anthem. Morgan putting his hand on Ria's waist.

When the anthem finished, in the darkness, he grabbed for her hand. Once the lights came on, they made their way to the door.

As they walked through the double doors, Morgan cast Ria a side glance. Something thumped hard in his chest. He panicked. For the first time in his life, he was in *love*.

*What did that mean?*

Suddenly he had an overwhelming urge for commitment. Both ways. But, when he looked at her smiling at him, he realised it was too soon. He didn't want to panic her into running.

Morgan would wait. He was a patient person - when it mattered. He'd just have to keep going out on dates with her, until she felt the same about him.

~~~~

After a couple of months of dating, Morgan could tell that Ria had finally become relaxed in his company. He couldn't wait any longer. The time had come to push Ria for some commitment.

He smiled drolly to himself. He wasn't a monk after all!

The last month had been hard. He wasn't satisfied with just her kisses anymore. He'd stopped sleeping properly because her face and body invaded his dreams, making his frustrations worse.

Now, he just needed to convince her to take their relationship to the next level. Legitimately. He wanted to marry her.

Not long after, Morgan broached the subject while they walked through town. "My parents are off to London for a long weekend. Do you think you would be able to stay over Friday night?" He asked hopefully, not sure if he was breathing properly. "Somewhere we'll not be interrupted?"

Ria stopped short. She was slightly shocked at his request. Hesitating, she glanced down at their hands.

*Surely, she trusted him enough to be alone with him? All alone, overnight?*

Panic rippled through her. If she said 'yes', he would be expecting more than just kisses and cuddles.

Ria took a breath to calm herself.

*Was she ready for this next step?*

She looked up into the blue of his eyes and watched him gaze intently at her, waiting for her answer. She sighed quietly. He had been very patient with her. She knew he wanted her — she wasn't that young that she hadn't felt his desire on many occasions.

Ria tried to swallow but found her mouth dry.

Ria?" Morgan prodded gently.

Taking a deep breath, she knew she was willing to take the leap. She wanted him. All of him. "I think so, I will arrange something with my parents."

Morgan's face lit up. He beamed from ear to ear.

*So, she was willing to make the next step to commit to him?*

Morgan knew what his next move was.

## Chapter 10

Megan was busy wiping her floury hands on her apron, while Evan sat in his usual position, at the table, reading the newspaper. "Would you like another mug of tea, Evan?"

Evan looked over his paper. "No thanks, love. You just carry on with what you are doing. By the way, it smells wonderful, as usual. Apple tart for tea is it, love?"

Megan smiled lovingly at her husband of twenty-five years. She cherished the times when he sat in the kitchen while she pottered around. Even though he was a man of few words, with his presence came the peace of mind that he was safe. Since the accident down the mines, what could have happened was on her mind too much.

A knock on the door interrupted her thoughts. She waited a second. If it were family or any of her friends, they would let themselves in after their knock. No one came through the door, so she finished wiping her hands, and went to see who wanted them this morning.

Megan felt a little flustered when she opened the door to find Morgan Templeton standing there.

She resisted the urge to run her hand through her hair to make sure it was fixed properly, as they were still too floury. "Oh, Mr Templeton. Please excuse all the flour. I'm in the middle of baking."

Morgan looked over her shoulder towards the kitchen. "Yes, I can smell something good." His gaze returned to Megan. "Would it be possible to come in and have a word with you and Mr Dillwyn? I took the liberty to find out that it was his day off. Is he here?"

"Oh, yes. Do come in." She stepped to the side to allow him entry, and then shouted from behind Morgan. "Evan, it is Mr Templeton, Ria's friend."

Morgan turned back toward Megan. "Please, call me Morgan."

Evan turned towards the door as Morgan came striding into the little kitchen, his hand outstretched for a handshake. What Evan didn't realise was that it wasn't confidence he was witnessing from Morgan, but a good show of someone trying to hide his nerves.

Evan, always a little unsure around people of money, forced himself to stand slowly, before offering his hand. "What can we do for you this fine morning?"

"Evan," Megan reprimanded her husband, a little flustered. "Mr Templeton... sorry, Morgan, might like a cup of tea or coffee before you talk?"

Morgan would have loved a cup of coffee, but his mouth was dry with nerves, and he knew he would probably spill it all down him, the way his hands were shaking. "No, thank you, Mrs Dillwyn. I might have a coffee after." He looked back at Evan. "After we have a talk." He did his best to ignore Evan's raise eyebrows.

"Sit," Evan offered as continued to study Morgan. Evan settled back into his chair, aware that Morgan looked somewhat uncomfortable. He narrowed his eyes, curious to know what had brought him here. Evan had to stifle the urge to smile - he couldn't say that he didn't get a kick at seeing the young, usually confident man, hot under the collar. Evan waited silently for Morgan to begin.

Morgan took a swift glance at Megan first, who had obviously busied herself at the stove in order for the men to talk. He took in a large breath and looked directly at Evan. "You know that I've been taking Ria out for a couple of months, now?"

"Yes, I am aware you have been seeing my daughter on a regular basis. What of it?" Evan paused. He sat up straighter. "She isn't in any trouble, is she?" Evan thought he knew his daughter well enough that she would come to them if she were in any trouble, but he wasn't going to make it easy on Morgan. He enjoyed seeing the flustered look that came over Morgan's face.

Megan stopped preparing the pot of tea, unable to pretend she wasn't curious about the conversation.

"Goodness, no!" Morgan spluttered before he caught Megan's eye. "I would like to ask your permission for Ria's hand in marriage."

This time is was Evan's time to be flustered.

Megan's face broke into a smile when she watched her darling husband digest the news that one of his children was going to get married.

Evan gasped out his reply. "Yes. Why, yes, of course." He got up swiftly and held out his hand to congratulate Morgan. "Megan, love. Get that whisky out, forget the coffee. We have some celebrating to do."

"Hopefully, I haven't asked her yet," laughed Morgan as he watched Evan fill up a glass with whisky.

It was going to be a long morning.

~~~~

"Yes, Mam. I'm catching a movie with Karen tonight, and I'm going to stay overnight." Ria nibbled her bottom lip with worry. She had never lied to her mother before, or anyone come to that.

*What on earth was she doing?*

She glanced at her mother from under her lashes, too guilty to elaborate on the conversation.

"Okay," said Megan.

Ria knew she should tell her parents the truth, that she was going to spend some time with Morgan, but she didn't think they would understand. They certainly wouldn't approve of her spending the night with him. She gave a defeated sigh. It would be useless to explain that she felt ready, that she was sure she loved him. It wouldn't matter – they were her parents.

Ria carried on eating her sandwich. Besides, it had been a strange week in the house. A little time away would be good. Her parents had been acting strangely. Giving each other secretive looks, and then smiling at her. She'd asked numerous times what was wrong, but they kept saying 'nothing'. It had just about sent her barmy. Something was up with them, but they weren't going to let her in on their secret.

She glanced at the clock on the mantle and wished Tom was home from work. She often talked through problems with her brother, mainly because he had the knack of making problems seem much better. She hoped he'd be back soon.

After she had put her plate in the sink, Ria made her way into the sitting room. She couldn't settle. She didn't like lying to her parents.

"Where's Tom, Mam?" Ria shouted through to the kitchen.

"I'm not sure. He should be back soon," Megan cried back. "Unless he's gone out the a girl," she mumbled.

Ria sighed. She wanted to check with Tom whether she *should* tell them where she was going. Ria knew they wouldn't be too happy, but this was the 50's, wasn't it? She was over the age of consent, and surely it was better to 'know' a man *before* you married them?

She shook her head to dislodge her fancy thoughts.

*Who was she kidding?*

First of all, modern ideas didn't work in a small community and, Morgan had never mentioned marriage. This was purely a physical thing.

Ria sat back down in an attempt to calm her nerves. She smoothed down her skirt. Spending time with Morgan was what she wanted to do, but she still wanted to ask Tom's advice.

*What were you supposed to feel when you were in love?*

She laughed nervously. Thinking about it seriously, she didn't know if Tom had ever got to that stage. The way he went through women, could he love any of them?

Ria knew she shouldn't kid herself. What she longed to know, but also dreaded asking Tom, was that if a woman slept with him did it make him 'go off' them, or did he still respect them?

If she was entirely honest, if Morgan did walk away after she slept with him, she would be broken and wouldn't know how she would cope.

Up until tonight, even though she'd had a wonderful couple of months with Morgan, every time things started to get past kissing, she backed off quickly. She knew what he ultimately wanted, but she hadn't been ready. He had never complained, though. He always respected her wishes.

But tonight, even though her mind still told her to be cautious, to remember the gossips, her heart told her to trust him.

She got up and paced, frustration taking hold. If she slept with him or not, she didn't think she would *ever* be the same again. No one would affect her like Morgan.

Stopping the urge to bite her nails, she wished for Tom again.

*Where was he? He was usually back by now.*

When Ria looked at the clock on the mantle again, she realised her time for chatting things over with him had gone.


Morgan sat in his car and waited. He was uncomfortable. It felt as though his heart was trying to escape from his chest, it was racing so much.

He attempted to relax his hands. At the moment, they were gripping the steering wheel.

*It was like being a teenager again. Waiting to pick up his first date!*

Morgan let out a quick snort. At least now, his car didn't have rust spots like his first one did. And, there would be no fumbling in the back seats of the car, either.

Morgan leant forward and switched on the radio, in an attempt to calm himself.  He was surprised how wound up he felt. But, then again, he'd never proposed to anyone before!

Morgan hoped he could make it a night to remember. His hand checked whether 'the box' was still safe in his jacket pocket.

A movement caught his eye. It was Ria, walking towards him carrying a small overnight bag.

*Yes, he felt like a teenager again!*

Morgan got out of the car to open the door for her. "Hello."

"Hello."

"You look beautiful, Ria," he murmured as he gently kissed her lips.

When he stepped back, Morgan noticed her familiar blush rise on her cheeks. She still wasn't entirely used to his compliments. He was determined that was going to change. He would make sure of it. "Your chariot awaits, my lady."

"Thank you." Ria slid into the luxurious cream interior of the car. While she watched Morgan walk around the front of the car, she took a deep breath to calm her nerves. He smiled at her when he noticed her watching him and her stomach did the funny little flop she had grown used to.

Morgan affected her in a way that no one had before. But, it was all so new, sometimes Ria found it hard to distinguish what she was experiencing. She only hoped her instincts about tonight were right.

*It was what she wanted, wasn't it? But what happened if she was wrong?*

Morgan slid into the car. He placed his hand on her leg.

Ria jumped under his palm.

Morgan sighed, she was still nervous. He kept his hand firmly on her leg and turned to give her a light kiss on her lips. He didn't want her to change her mind about staying tonight, so he changed the subject. "I hope you are hungry. I have a made a feast."

After Ria had given him a shaky smile, he started the engine, eager to get her home. "Your parents are okay with you staying over?"

Ria swallowed the feeling of discomfort.

*Why on earth had she started this lie? Why hadn't she been honest with her parents, and Morgan, too?*

Ria knew him enough to know that he would not be happy if he found out her parents didn't know she was with him. Her only option was to skirt around the subject without lying. . She looked at his profile from beneath her lowered eyelashes. "They told me to have a nice night." She looked away. She wasn't technically lying, they had told her to have a nice evening, but obviously they thought she was going out with Karen.

Morgan put the car into gear and pulled out into a space in the traffic. "Come on, then. I'm starving."

Tom was tired. Work at the indoor market had not been a bundle of laughs recently. There had been a sickness bug, and he had to work extra shifts to compensate.

As he walked home, he gave himself a tired smile. Despite his tiredness, after his mother's food, he was off out with Holly. A lady that he'd met at his local, the Red Lion. They had flirted with each other for a couple of months, and at long last, he was taking her out. Tired or not. The thought of his date put the spring back in his step.

When Tom reached the kerb, he stopped and checked both ways, ready to cross the road. A familiar looking car caught his eye.

As it whizzed by, Tom caught sight of the recognisable colour of his sister's hair. Her head thrown back in a laugh.

Tom rolled his shoulders, suddenly becoming agitated. Obviously, that Templeton man was keeping her entertained. He quickened his step, wanting to get home faster.

Tom hadn't even hung his coat up before he started to question his mother. "Mam, where's Ria off to, tonight?"

Megan turned around from the sink and smiled at her son. "Oh, she's going with Karen to the cinema. Staying over too, as it is the weekend. Why, love?"

"Karen?" Tom questioned, confused.

*That certainly wasn't Karen.*

"Why, what's wrong?"

"Nothing, Mam. Just thought I saw her earlier on." His stomach clenched. It was unlike Ria to lie to their Mam.

"Oh, okay," said Megan as she turned back to draining the boiled potatoes.

Suddenly, Tom found himself hot under the collar. He was uncomfortable with his thoughts about her evening. *He* knew what he'd been thinking about Holly, surely that Templeton guy would have those same feelings about his sister?

He glanced at his brothers, who sat at the table, waiting for their food.  Tom suddenly knew why he was unsettled. Morgan was an experienced man. A man with more than kissing on his mind.

Ria stepped into the living room at Morgan's parent's house.  Its lights were turned down low. She gasped. It wasn't like anything she was expecting. It was entirely different from her traditional family house, full of modern furniture, the likes of which she had only seen in Karen's magazines before. Everywhere she looked was plastic, Formica, and plywood.

Out of nowhere, Ria felt uncomfortable again.

*How different their backgrounds and experiences were.*

Looking around she realised the Templetons were very wealthy to afford fashionable, up-to-date furniture.

"Okay?" Morgan said as he walked into the room after hanging up their coats.

"Hmm," she replied walking further into the room. Ria tried to shake off the feeling. She didn't want to think of their differences, not at the moment. She was already nervous enough.

Ria glanced around, trying to find something to start up a conversation. "You have a TV." She walked over to the set that sat in the corner of the room.

"Yes," said Morgan, a little confused by her enthusiasm.

Ria bent down and noticed her reflection in the convex screen. She smiled as she swivelled to look at him. "Perhaps we can watch it later on?"

*It was the last thing he wanted to do!*

"Perhaps," he said. Morgan shook his head to clear his thoughts. He looked back at her, enjoying the excitement in her eyes. It beat the unsure look she had moments before. "My mother *had* to have it to watch the Coronation of Queen Elizabeth." He stuck his hands in his pocket. "About four years ago now. My poor father couldn't put up with her nagging anymore. I don't think I have heard her nag so much. Well, since she wanted a washing machine, that is."

Ria's mouth rounded in astonishment. "A washing machine, too? You're lucky." She stood up and brushed her fingers along the top of the television set. "All we got for the Coronation was the extra pound of sugar, and the four ounces of margarine they gave out on top of our usual rations." She grinned at him over her shoulder, while she walked away. "Although, Mam did make an amazing cake with the extra goodies."

She walked over to the large window, overlooking their garden. She heaved a sigh. The war had finished, but she still remembered that rationing had been in place for a while after. It had been hard for everyone.

Ria twirled away from the window. She smiled, determined to enjoy herself, not wallow on life's hardships.

She spotted a black, leather chair with shiny moulded plywood. "What an amazing chair. Your father's, I assume?"

Morgan nodded.

"Can I try it?"

"Of course, go ahead. Mother had it sent from America for my father's 50th Birthday. Apparently, it's an *Eames* lounger, not that it means anything to me."

It didn't mean anything to Ria, either.

She carefully lowered herself into it, picking up her feet and placing them onto the ottoman that accompanied it. She pushed back into its comfort. "I could get used to this," she gave a giggle. She stretched her arms into the air.

It was like watching a child in a playground. Ria was so fascinated by all the modern furniture. Morgan was pleased. He personally didn't like all the bright colours, but as long as she liked it. He wanted her to be happy.

The smile faded from his lips. A powerful feeling of desire passed through him. He looked away quickly. Now wasn't the time.

Ria glanced up at Morgan. She thought she witnessed something flitter across his eyes.

*What was it?*

She became confused when he quickly looked towards the window. Becoming more uncomfortable, Ria got up from the chair.

When Morgan had calmed enough, he turned to look at her. He noticed that she had got up from the chair.

Cursing under his breath, he realised that his actions had made her close down again. "Come on, let's go into the kitchen."

He walked over to her and gently took her hand. He led her through the door leading into the kitchen.

If Ria noticed the new Formica kitchen that his mother had just had fitted, Morgan was quietly pleased she did not mention anything. He wanted her to feel at home, not intimidated again.

Set off in one corner of the room was a lovely table that had been set with silverware and plates.

Noticing the table, Ria strolled over to it. She ran her fingers along the delicate tablecloth.

"Is it okay?" Morgan asked, a little unsure of her quietness.

She turned around to face him. "You did all this for me?"

"Well, I did have a little help," he replied.

He stepped forward and pulled out a seat for her.

When she was settled, Morgan picked up a bottle of wine. He turned the label towards Ria. "Is the wine good enough for you, my lady?" he teased, trying to use his best waiter's voice.

"I have no idea. But I'm sure it is." Ria watched as he poured two glasses.

He handed one to her.

Morgan watched her intently, trying to gauge her happiness. As her lips touched the rim of the glass, he cursed quietly under his breath. His attention had been drawn to her mouth, and he wanted to kiss them. Before desire took hold, he turned towards the kitchen. "Wait there, your starter is coming up."

The food was delicious and the company enjoyable. Ria was sure her ribs hurt from all the laughter they shared during the meal. They had mostly reminisced about their childhoods - each having funny tales to recall.

Once the chocolate dessert was consumed, Morgan led Ria to sit on the sofa.

Soft classical music played on a record in the background.

Ria didn't know the music, but it was relaxing.

"You don't know how many times I have pictured you sitting on here with me," said Morgan.

"Oh, have you?" she whispered, a little unsure of what to say.

"Yes." Morgan refilled her wine glass and replaced the bottle on the side table. He turned back to her. "I haven't been able to get you out of my mind since the Christmas kiss under that mistletoe." He watched a blush colour her cheeks. He'd hoped his honest feelings would relax her, make her know how much he thought of her.

"Oh."

Morgan noticed a slight tremble of her hand holding the glass. "You looked so beautiful. You took my breath away." He reached out and gently pushed her hair behind her ear. Unable to break their contact, he continued to softly run his fingers over her earlobe and down her neck.

Ria tried to keep still and not fidget, but his light touch sent tingles all through her. As she attempted to keep her emotions in check, she picked on a subject that deflated her growing feelings. "But you had come with that beautiful blonde lady. She was gorgeous," she blurted out.

Ria felt silly when she noticed Morgan suppress a smile.

"Mary? Is that jealousy I detect?" he teased. He moved his hand from her neck and slowly started to slide out her hairpins, one by one.

"No, I ...um." Ria kicked herself for not finding a suitable answer. The touch of his hands made it hard to think.

Morgan's piercing blue eyes narrowed. Even though she was the one here with him, she had a confused look in her eye again. "Let me assure you that *you* are the one I want, *no* one else." A smile flickered on his lips when she finally glanced back at him. "You are the most beautiful woman I have ever seen. You are the one I dream of making love to. No one else."

"Oh," was all she could squeak out.

With his free hand, Morgan gently took away the wine glass that Ria held in front of her like a shield. He turned and placed it next to his on the coffee table.

When he swivelled back to face her, he leant forward and gently placed a warm, wine-flavoured kiss on her lips.

Ria sighed.

"You don't know how long I have looked forward to doing that." He touched her lips again. "I spend my waking hours wanting to kiss your beautiful lips, and I spend my dreams being haunted by them."

Ria tried to swallow.

Morgan lightly kissed along her jaw to her ear. He whispered, "I am so happy you are going to be spending a night with me."

Ria felt panic rise, despite his fingertips on the back of her neck sending shivers of desire down her spine. She was glad he couldn't see her face.

Morgan felt her stiffen in his arms despite his efforts. "Don't be frightened, darling. I will never do anything to hurt you," he whispered, before kissing a path down to the fluttering pulse in her neck.

"I know," she whispered.

"Good." Although it was killing him, Morgan knew he had to go slow. He needed the opportunity to show her the softer side of loving.

Over the months of waiting for her, he'd decided that when the time came, he wouldn't rush her. He needed to make sure it was what she wanted as well. Morgan didn't want her to have any regrets after. He wouldn't.

He was glad he had the foresight to ask her parents for permission to marry her. All he had to do now was to wait for the right time to ask her.

Ria relaxed, enjoying the feather light kisses Morgan placed over her face and neck. As each new increasing wave of ecstasy washed over her, Ria became more pliable to his touch.

Morgan knew she was starting to unwind and enjoy herself. The rapid beat of her heart matched his own. Once he saw her eyes drift shut in pleasure, his physical desire moved up a level. He possessively returned his lips to hers.

Sensing the change in gear, Ria started to panic again. She knew this night wasn't just about loving kisses. This was leading to much more.

Suddenly, Ria felt hot and overwhelmed.

She broke away from his deep kiss. "Wait," she murmured, unsure if he'd heard her.

Morgan carried on kissing her neck.

Ria wasn't sure if she was ready yet. She tried to pull back, emotionally and physically.

Somewhere in the back of his mind, Morgan felt her still in his embrace. Putting his raging desires to the side, he stopped. "What's wrong, darling?" He used his finger to gently lift her face to look at him. His gaze narrowed as he saw the flush of passion in her cheeks, and her red lips, swollen from his kisses. "What's wrong? Am I hurting you?"

"I, no, it's just…" Ria struggled to look at him.

"What, just tell me?" he coaxed.

She knew that her cold feet were silly. Before she'd come, she understood what Morgan expected from her if she stayed the night. But suddenly, it didn't matter what she'd told herself - she felt young and foolish.

She tried to avoid his gaze, pulling away from his finger. Ria bit her bottom lip nervously.

*What would he think of her? He had told her numerous times that he wanted her, but did he love her?*

Morgan recognised her case of nerves. He gently talked to her, trying to alleviate her anxieties.

Ria started to relax.

"I want you like I've never wanted anyone before."

Ria flinched.

*There was that want again.*

Unsure of what he'd said to upset her, Morgan watched as uncertainty flickered over her face. He pushed a hand through his hair. Apparently he wasn't using the right words.

He tried again. "But I also know you are old fashioned in your views."

Ria winced. That statement hurt Ria. It made her feel very young and childish.

*What did he want, a more experienced woman?*

Ria sat up in an attempt of trying to control her feelings.

Morgan cursed. He couldn't seem to get it right.

*Why wasn't this going the way he intended?*

The last thing he wanted was to hurt Ria.

Unsure of what to do, he let her move away from him a little.   Wary, he watched as apprehension flicked across her face. When she chewed her bottom lip, and looked as though she was going to cry, he placed his finger back under her chin and kissed the end of her nose.

So far, he hadn't done a good job, but Morgan was going to rectify the situation. "Hey listen, Ria. It's nothing to be frightened or ashamed of."

She glanced away.

"Please look at me." He waited until she did. "I want more than *that*. I love you, Ria. More than words can describe." He watched her lip tremble. "But perhaps actions are better?"

Ria watched as he got off the sofa. He reached for his jacket, which lay on the back of it. She continued to watch as he reached into the pocket and bought out a navy small box.

When he kneeled in front of her, her heart fluttered.

"I would like you to become my wife."

When Morgan opened the box, she saw a diamond, solitaire ring. She couldn't speak.

Morgan's eyes narrowed, watching for her reaction. "It was my Grandmother's," he explained, suddenly becoming nervous at her lack of response. Butterflies battered around inside him.

*What happened if she didn't like it? Or worse still - what happened if she refused?*

"If you don't like it, you can choose something else."

Ria glanced up from the ring and stared wide-eyed at him. She hadn't expected this! Shock rippled through her system. "I...I... it's beautiful ...I ...um ..." Her hands reached towards the box, and then, as if burnt, she clasped them to her chest trying to stop them shaking.

Morgan recognised the panicked look on her face. From bended knee, he took one of her trembling hands. Straightening her finger, he placed the ring on it. "Victoria Dillwyn, will you do me the great honour of becoming my wife?"

Tears sprang into her eyes. "Yes, yes of course," she blurted out. She pulled him up and wrapped her arms around his neck.

As they kissed, tears of happiness fell down her cheeks.

Her head swam - he loved her *and* wanted to marry her. It seemed too good to be true - all her fantasies wrapped into one.

Morgan pulled away and inspected the ring, now firmly on her finger. His eyes misted with tears. He was so happy. "It is a little big for you."

"It's lovely."

"Your fingers are much smaller than my Grandmother. But, I'll have it made smaller." He stopped talking for a second and looked at her. "That is, if you like this one and don't want a new one?"

Ria fingered the ring. It was a little loose, but she loved it. Loved it even more because it was special to Morgan. "This one is just wonderful. I wouldn't want any other one."

"Great, I'll have it made smaller for you this week."

Giving it one last look, Ria reluctantly took it off and placed it back into the box.

Morgan snapped the lid closed. He put it on the side table. When he turned around, Ria slipped her hands around his neck and played with the thickness of his black hair. He didn't resist when he felt her pull his mouth towards hers. He wanted her.

Ria wanted to feel close to him. Experiencing an overwhelming sense of joy, she wanted to share her happiness with him. She craved those new feelings of desire to be released in her body again.

This time, there was no hesitation.

Pulling Ria onto the sofa with him, he kissed her. Deepening his kisses, he angled his body, manoeuvring her along the chair. Using his bent arms behind her head, he tried not to crush her under his weight.

When she used her hands to pull him closer, heat crept into him and raged through his bloodstream. Everywhere his hard body came into contact with her soft form, felt so right.

*She'd agreed to be his wife!*

Morgan was experienced enough to know that he couldn't wait much longer. But, he didn't want her first time to be on a sofa. He broke his kiss. "Let's take this to the bedroom," he whispered into her ear.

"Hmmm."

Morgan slowly untangled her arms and stood up. He offered her his hand. He smiled at her when she took hold of it.

Turning, he led her up the stairs.

When they arrived, Ria looked around the bedroom. She tried to take in its features, in an attempt to steady her breathing.

It was a masculine room, one mainly of dark blues. Her previous nervousness reappeared when she noticed the bed. She pressed her hands on her stomach in an effort to stop the fluttering.

Breathing deeply, she reminded herself that he wanted to marry her. This was not a sordid little fling.

Morgan bent and switched on the side lights. He noticed Ria place her hands on her stomach. Her nervousness was back.

Morgan walked over to her, slowly, not to spook her. When he reached her, he gave her a gentle hug before he kissed her temple. He smiled into her hair when he felt Ria sigh. "I'm not going to push you. Are you sure about this?" he whispered between his kisses. "Even though I think it will kill me, you can change your mind." Morgan desperately hoped that she wouldn't.

"Yes, I'm sure..." Even though her voice was a little shaky, there was love and determination in her eyes.

Soundlessly, Morgan manoeuvred Ria towards his bed. With their lips locked, he gently eased her back on the bed and sank into the mattress beside her.

Her eyes closed. She shuddered.

Morgan's mouth let go of hers and wandered over her face towards her neck.

The caress of his lips made her move, giving him easier access. It tickled, but felt so good.

Before long, his wandering kisses returned to possess her mouth. His warm tongue gently ran back and forth across hers, waiting for her to open up for him. Once she did, he changed his angle, to allow deeper access.

Her tongue joined his and twisted.

Morgan felt her heat of her body through their clothes. He wanted to touch her delicate, pale skin. He couldn't wait any longer. Carefully, he started to slip her clothes off, one button at a time.

Ria's body felt as though it had hot lava running through its veins. Everywhere his hands touched her turned sweetly hot. Somewhere in the depths of her mind, she recognised that his nimble fingers had slowly undone each button of her blouse. At that moment, she didn't care. Her clothes felt like an unwanted barrier. She'd wanted to discard them as much as he did. The burning heat of her blood getting too much to bear.

As he paid her attention, Ria couldn't think correctly, but she trusted him enough to follow wherever he wanted to take her.

When Morgan parted her blouse, he paused. Ria's translucent skin reminded him of velvet. He noticed her quiver.

"Morgan?" she whispered, unsure of why he had stopped?

*Did he like what he saw?*

He smiled, bending his head down to place a kiss on her chest. Wanting her to relax, he moved back to her mouth, giving it more attention.

While they kissed, Ria felt Morgan's hand move over her rib cage. It felt warm as he left it there for a while.

When Morgan sensed her relaxing, he broke off their kiss, moving down her body. He was determined to kiss the alabaster skin of her body. As his mouth moved down, trailing kisses, one of his hands gently cupped her breast in its cradle. He felt her breast swell, as he took its weight.

"Morgan," she moaned.

He moved his head level with his hand. He kneaded her, and was desperate to give it some. He rose over her breast and bent his head. Removing his hand, he slid his tongue along their swells. Eventually he ran his tongue under the edge of her bra, teasing her into hard peaks.

Ria thought she was going to go mad with longing for him. Heat pooled low in her stomach. Wriggling, she frantically needed to relieve the pressure growing there. But she didn't know how.

"Can I take it off, Ria?" Morgan glanced up at her, waiting for her permission.

He waited for her to nod.

Ria couldn't talk, but she could help. Reaching around her back, she helped Morgan remove the offending article. She groaned deeply as he took her into his warm mouth. A pull shot straight through down her as she crushed his head against her body.

Crazy with sensations and not sure what she was supposed to do, Ria pulled his head back up to her lips.

She didn't know what to do, but she wanted to touch him, too. Send *him* crazy with desire.

While they kissed, Ria slid her hand under his open shirt. She groaned into his mouth when she reached the hot, taut muscles on his back.

Not being able to wait any longer, all their garments were swiftly removed and tossed on the floor.

Morgan extended his arms either side of her head and gazed down at her naked form.

Ria felt embarrassed. She tried to cover herself with her arms.

He rolled onto his side, leaning his head on his hand. "Don't. I want to look at you. You're beautiful." He used his free hand to draw circles on her flat stomach.

Ria closed eyes and stayed still. She was determined not to move, but too self-conscious to look directly at him.

"Look at me, my love," Morgan whispered.

Keeping them shut, she shook her head. "I can't."

"Please." He pushed up and covered her body with his. "Look at me, Ria."

Ria opened them slowly, happy that her body was now not on show. She watched his descending mouth. She wanted him. All of him. She knew she was ready to give herself to him. Instinctively, her legs wrapped around his.

Morgan pulled away from their kiss. "You know that I want to make love to you?"

"Yes," she whispered.

"Do you want me, too?" His voice was low and husky as desire filled his request.

Ria looked deep into his eyes. They told her everything she needed to know.     "Yes. Yes, I do."

That's all he needed to hear.

## Chapter 11

Morgan switched off the car engine. They were a street away from Ria's house. He wanted to take her all the way to her door, to see her parents, but Ria had insisted that he dropped her off here. "Are you sure I can't drive you nearer?"

Ria grabbed her bag close to her chest. "No, thanks. This is fine. I'd like a little walk." She certainly didn't want her parents to see his car. There would be too many questions.

"Okay." Morgan smiled, not thinking any more about it. He was in too good a mood, having had her wake up next to him. He'd got such a kick watching her before she'd awoken. She'd looked so peaceful.

Morgan had asked her to stay the whole weekend, but she seemed determined to get home. Not wanting to seem too possessive, Morgan didn't push her. He knew there would be plenty of other times that they could enjoy each other again. His smile increased as he remembered their enjoyment.

"What's wrong?" she gave him a wary smile.

Morgan shrugged. "Just remembering last night." He leant forward to play with her blouse opening.

"Oh," she said, a little embarrassed.

When he noticed her glance around, presumably checking that no one was around, Morgan pulled his hand away. He didn't want to embarrass her in public.

*Perhaps he could persuade her for more private time, tomorrow?*

"Remember. Tomorrow, 10 o'clock at the beach. I'll bring something to eat because my parents left too much in the fridge." Morgan's eyes narrowed. "Okay?" It concerned him that she was keeping her eyes averted from him and was worrying her bottom lip. She looked vulnerable as she sat there, silently.

*What was wrong? How could she look so unsure, after what they shared last night and this morning?*

He leant over the handbrake, trying to get closer to her. "What's wrong, darling?" He waited until she glanced at him. "Hey, don't look so sad. Will you meet me tomorrow?" He cupped his hands around her face, and gently kissed her lips.

Ria felt a surge of tenderness as some of her nervousness slipped away. She brought her lips up to meet his, desperately hoping that he wouldn't see the tears misting her eyes.

To be truthful, since they had slept together, reality had hit. Last night, her emotions took the lead, but now morning had come, she was scared that he was done with her.

As everyone had warned her.

Ria pulled away from his kiss very slowly. She noticed his gaze flick to her mouth before he looked into her eyes.

*No, she was being silly.*

"So will you meet me?"

"Yes," she replied, leaning forward for another kiss.

*He'd asked her to marry him, so why on earth was she having doubts?* Perhaps it was nerves because she'd been dishonest to her family, and she had to face them this morning.

*Would she tell them the truth, or continue the farce?*

Her conscious didn't sit well. Pulling away from his embrace, she saw the concern on his face. Her fears slipped away. "Yes, I'll meet you at 10."

"Great." He sighed.

Ria knew what she was going to do. She was going to tell her parents about last night. Tell them that she'd stayed with him and that they were going to get married. "I'll wait on the beach for you. I'll bring something to drink." She kissed him lightly.

He wasn't letting her off that easily. He grabbed the back of her head to deepen the kiss.

A while later, Morgan moved his lips to nibble the corner of her lips. "You'd better go now. Before I can't let you go and take you back home."

She giggled.

Morgan waved his hands and laughed. "I mean it. Run along now," Morgan teased. He reached over her to open her car door.

"Okay, I'm going."

Morgan planted one more kiss on the tip of her nose before she turned.

He watched her scurry out of the car.

She turned and waved.

"Remember, I love you," Morgan shouted out of his window.

When she was out of site, he started the car and drove off. He felt wonderful.

Initially, he hadn't wanted to take Ria home. He wanted to spend the weekend with her - he wanted to spend the rest of his life with her.

But, at the moment, he couldn't, so he'd just have to be content with meeting her at the beach.

Driving along, he glanced in the side mirror. He laughed at his good mood. Ria had got him in this mood. No one had done that to him before. His emotions were so different to anything he'd experienced before, he knew categorically that he loved her. The squeeze of his heart, the flip of his stomach when he thought of her, he'd never felt as content before.

When Morgan arrived and opened the front door, the ringing of the house phone brought him out of his thoughts.

He quickly strode over and picked it up.

"Hey, Morgan. It's Darren. You need to get up to London, now. Father has had a stroke. We don't know if he is going to make it..."

~~~~

Morgan paced the hospital corridor with a forgotten cup of cold coffee in his hand.

Emptiness engulfed him. He glanced at his mother who sat silently staring into thin air. Darren had a comforting arm around her, his coffee also forgotten by his feet.

Over the hours, faceless people came and went. People waiting for their own news, also in dreamlike states that were so prevalent in hospitals.

The footsteps of nurses, the faint smell of antiseptics, and the far-off crying of relatives were all effectively shut out by Morgan. Even though his mind was foggy, it raced all over the place.

So far, the news wasn't good. His father had suffered another stroke while in the theatre. It was hours later, but they still didn't know if he was going to pull through.

Morgan pushed his fingers through his hair and rubbed the back of his neck. He knew he was too tense for the kneading of his fingers to make any difference, but it was something to do.

Morgan felt angry, annoyed, useless. All emotions he wasn't comfortable with.

Glancing towards his mother again, sadness and annoyance battled within him. Throwing his cup away, he pushed his hands in his pockets. He sighed heavily.

Apart from his father's illness, Morgan was also reeling from his mother's admission that the Swansea factory didn't have any trouble.

Between themselves, they had decided they wanted Morgan back home to *marry* Mary. And to take an interest in the factory. They wanted it to become his – his, Mary's, and their children.

He let out a short breath.

*No wonder he hadn't found any discrepancies in the paperwork he'd pored over for hours.*

He turned away from her.

*How could his parents have lied to him?*

Morgan knew they hinted about grandchildren, and Darren was nowhere near, but did that give them the right to meddle in his life?

Morgan's jaw tensed. He blew out a breath of frustration at the whole mess.

He'd enjoyed a good life in London, why bring him back under false pretences? His parents had brought him up to honest – what a farce that was. And, what a waste of time it was in Swansea, or was it?

Morgan knew, deep down, that he wouldn't have met Ria if he were still in London.

He sighed. Looking back at her, Morgan knew now wasn't the time or the place to confront her. She had enough on her plate. His mother was so wrapped up in grief, she wasn't aware of how uncomfortable her surroundings were.

His heart constricted painfully. He loved them both, and understood that they'd done it with good intentions, He decided to keep his frustrations to himself, and spare his mother the extra worry. Besides, she must have felt sorry about their deceit because it was nearly the first thing she had said to him when he arrived.

Morgan rubbed his chin, vaguely aware of stubble irritating his fingers. He knew the direction he wanted his life to go. Whether he had his parents blessing or not, he was going to marry someone he loved. And, as much as he liked Mary, he didn't love her.

They would just have to accept that.

Whatever happened, he wanted Ria beside him forever.

Now, all he had to do was make sure his father got well enough to meet his future wife, and hopefully, many grandchildren.

After a brief chat with the doctors and receiving no satisfactory answers, Morgan fought hard to keep the wave of helpless agitation at bay.

Making matter worse, Morgan had not had time to let Ria know what happened. He was supposed to meet her today on the beach. He cursed. Her family didn't have a phone in their house so that he could ring her.

Rattling his brain for a solution, he remembered Ria telling him that their neighbour had one that everyone along the street used. If he contacted the factory, he would be able to get a number from Andrew Jones.

As he checked his pockets for change, he realised it was the weekend.  There wouldn't be anyone at the factory until Monday. He pushed his fingers through his hair in total weariness.

*What would Ria think when he didn't turn up at the beach, tomorrow?*

Suddenly, Morgan panicked. She was already nervous about it. He cursed loudly, ignoring the stares he received. There was nothing he could do. He only hoped that Ria wouldn't doubt his love for her. He had expressed them clearly enough.

*Hadn't he?*

## Chapter 12

"What's wrong with you? You look as though you have been partying all weekend. Hey, girls. Look at the bags under Ria's eyes."

Ria forced a half-hearted smile. "Funny," she murmured.

Ria had dreaded coming back to work after the weekend. How could she tell them that it was crying and lack of sleep, not a fabulous weekend out partying, that caused her pale look?

She forced the lump in her throat away. The weekend had not gone to plan.

When she had arrived home from Morgan's, ready to confess to her parents, the house was full of relatives. So, she decided to put off their talk until after she had met him on the beach.

She'd waited excitedly, both nervous and anxious about seeing him again. But, Ria knew that when she saw him again, all her doubts and fears about what they had done would disappear.

*But he never appeared.*

As her workmates continued with their banter, she ignored them, hoping they would drop the subject if she looked uninterested.

*He never appeared!*

The familiar sick feeling was back. How could she begin to describe the heartbreak she felt, standing alone on the beach for hours waiting for Morgan to turn up? How could she bear to hear the *'told you so'* if she mentioned anything? How could she be so silly to believe he wanted to marry her? He hadn't even given her the ring. It was in its box at his house.

*Perhaps he did that to all his lovers to get them into bed?*

Ria shuddered, her confidence in their romance shaken to the foundation.

Glancing at the smiling faces around her, Ria decided it was better for her colleagues to think that she had been partying. For as long as she could keep the pretence going.

The supervisor's voice broke through her thoughts. "Hey, Mr Jones had just mentioned that old Mr Templeton had a stroke over the weekend. Not in a good way, they say."

Ria felt her breath catch. Blood rushed back into her pale face. She fought the urge to ask any question – she didn't want to sound too eager. She was, after all, just an employee.

Waiting with the others for news, ideas ran through her head quickly. She had trouble making them out.

*Perhaps that is why Morgan did not turn up?*

Ria's restless fingers twisted her overall. Her teeth worried her bottom lip.  She hoped so.

Marge's booming voice made her jump. "What about Morgan Templeton? Will he be giving us an update today?"

From the distance, Ria heard the reply.

"They say he has gone back to London. After his father had a stroke, they said that he was needed up in the London factory. Rumour has it that he isn't coming back here..."

Ria felt a fog descend in front of her eyes. The room began to spin.

*How could I have been so silly? He has had his fun and now gone back to his life in London.*

Ria ran for the bathroom.

"Look at Victoria, running for the bathroom. It looks as though all that partying has made her want to throw up!" Her workmates chuckled, before turning back to their work.


Ria glanced at herself in the cracked bathroom mirror.

Bending forward, she turned on the tap. Cupping the water, she wet her face. She watched the water mix with her tears and disappear down the hole of the yellow stained sink.

Finally, Ria pulled herself out of her stupor. Quickly wiping her tears with the back of her hand, she took a deep breath. She tried to get some control, but arguments continued to whirl around in her head, making her lightheaded.

*It's your own fault. Everyone warned you about men like him - take their fun and then disappear.*

She grabbed the sink, her knuckles turning white.

*He'd seemed different. So loving, so giving. He told her he wanted her as his wife!*

Doubts crept in again. But he hadn't given her the ring.

*Is that what men did to trick women into bed?*

Morgan told her he loved her, hadn't he? Or were they easy words for him to say? She sighed heavily, realising she didn't have the experience to know. Her chest tightened with anxiety.

Glancing at the mirror again, her fingers gripped harder for support. Whatever happened, she knew she loved him. Even though she wasn't experienced, she actually believed that he loved her too.

*There must be a mistake.*

Ria tried to think logically.

*Did he mention he was leaving?* No.

Perhaps he didn't know. His father had a stroke, after all. It would have been totally unexpected.

She swallowed as dread gripped her again.

*But why hadn't he got hold of her to tell her? Didn't she mean enough for him to get in touch with her, somehow?*

As her tears started to fall faster, she slid down the wall onto the floor. She sobbed into her hands.

## Chapter 13

For Morgan, the weeks snowballed into one frustration after another.

He'd had enough. Between sorting out the London factory, dealing with doctors and their medical jargon, his father making progress and then regressing – it was getting too much.

To top it all, Andrew Jones hadn't come back to him with Ria's neighbours phone number. Morgan was frustrated, but he couldn't make a fuss because nobody knew about their relationship.

Every time he attempted to tell his parents about his intentions to marry Ria, something or someone had got in the way. Even his brother, Darren.

He'd gone to Swansea to retrieve some clothes for his father, and cosmetics for his mother, but he'd also brought Mary back with him. Morgan's jaw tensed - just what he needed!

Mary was in the hospital room now, with his father.

Morgan glanced at her while she read a book to his father. He was still, but Mary insisted that he could hear her read.

Morgan sighed at the situation, knowing he was being ungrateful. Mary was a great help. Her presence allowed his mother to get some much-needed rest, and Mary was a soothing companion to spend the evening hours with, in their London house, when he was not sitting with his father.

Morgan looked out of the window at the carpark below.

Nevertheless, he wanted to be with Ria. The emptiness of not being around her was eating at him. "I'm just popping out a minute, Mary," Morgan said to her. He turned abruptly to leave the hospital room.

Mary looked up from the book. She faltered over the words. Mary had known, and loved, Morgan long enough to know that his mind was not on her. She continued reading to David.

Morgan decided that action was needed. It was pointless being annoyed with Andrew Jones. It didn't matter to Andrew that he'd asked for Ria's neighbour's number over two weeks ago. Besides, he'd hadn't made it sound urgent because Ria had asked him not to tell anyone at work about them until her parents knew.

Morgan cursed. He wished he had told Ria that he'd already asked her father and mother for her hand in marriage. He hadn't thought it was important to tell her until she'd spoken to her parents herself. He had respected her wishes, but it certainly wasn't making it easy to get the phone number.

Morgan placed money in the slot and rang Andrew Jones.

When he answered, impatience laced Morgan's voice. "Andrew, it's Morgan. Did you manage to get Victoria Dillwyn's neighbours number for me?" He felt exasperation flit through him, when he heard Jones shuffling through papers.

"Yes, yes, it is here somewhere. Sorry, I thought my secretary had given it to you... mmmm... ah, yes, here it is..."

Morgan wrote down the number on the back of his hand. After briefly asking if everything was going well with the factory, and updating him on his father, Morgan put the phone down and got ready to ring Ria's neighbour.


"You're such a good boy to me, Tom. Like a son, yes you are, like a son," Doris shouted from the kitchen as she arranged a pot of tea, and homemade cookies, on a plate. "I never would have known how to deal with that leak. If it weren't for you, my bathroom would be flooded by now."

Tom smiled to himself and seated himself down on a chair by the table. He scanned the room, full of Doris's knick-knacks. It felt good to help people. He sighed.

*Perhaps that's why he'd been feeling out of sorts, agitated for just over the last week?*

He'd gone to have a chat with Ria, about when he saw her in the car with Morgan. He'd wanted to sort out things with her, have a chat. On one hand, he was going to give her holy hell for lying to their Mam, but on the other, he was going to find out exactly what was going on between her and that Templeton man.

But, when he had gone to talk to her, he had been faced with a shut bedroom door and the sound of her sobbing behind it.

Every day he had gone to see Ria. Every day he faced the same scenario.

As each day passed, Tom became more uncomfortable with Ria's sadness and angrier with Morgan Templeton for being the apparent cause of his sister's distress. Tom had never been comfortable with tears, even though he had sisters, so it was easier to let the anger for Morgan grow instead.

Troubled by her mood, Tom had spoken to his mother. But, even though he had seen concern in her eyes, she'd told him not to get involved - Ria would talk to them when she was ready.

Tom hoped that Templeton hadn't hurt her, but with all her crying and closed off moods, he was inclined to think he had.

*Just wait until I got hold of him!*

The ring of Doris's phone interrupted his thoughts.

"Get that for me, would you, dear? I am just getting the last of the cookies out of the oven."

"Okay." Tom rose from the chair and strolled over to the phone. He picked the receiver up, and shook the money box that neighbours put money in when they asked to use Doris's phone. "Hello, Doris's residence. Tom speaking."

"Hi. Is that Tom? Ria's brother?" Relief poured through Morgan. He was going to be able to contact her at last.

"Yes, it is. Who's calling?" Tom curled the phone wire around his fingers. Of course he knew who it was, he just was not going to make it easy for the jerk who'd upset his sister.

"It's Morgan… Morgan Templeton. Could you give Ria a message for me?"

Tom didn't say anything.

"Just tell her that I had to go to London. I don't know how long I have to be up here." Morgan wanted to add that he missed her like crazy, but as he was talking to her brother, he didn't.

"That's all?" Tom asked.

"Yes, that is all. Thank you. Tell Ria I will ring her next week at the same time. Hopefully, she will be able to take the call?"

"I'll tell her. Bye." Tom put the phone down rather forcefully.

Tom's forehead creased.

Did he tell Ria that Morgan called and wanted to speak to her?  Did he risk him hurting her again?  Or should he *not* tell her, and give her time to get over him?

Tom hated seeing how upset Ria had been because of *something* that Templeton had done to her.  Even his parents were walking on eggshells around her.

He fell in and out of love quickly, she could, too.

*Give Ria a couple of weeks without him and she'll be back to normal.*


The alarm was like a monotonous banging in her head.  Ria fumbled to turn it off and silently cursing that she'd forgotten to switch if off.

Dragging her eyelids open, Ria stared at the ceiling. She noticed little cobwebs hanging from light shade.

The room was silent. Anne had already got left to do her paper round.

Ria sighed deeply. Another day to get through. But, at least, it was the weekend.  She wouldn't have to go to work, hoping that Morgan would show up.

He never did.

Ria sighed again. After a couple of months, she'd hoped to forget him. Hoped that the pain she felt all the time, would dim.  But it hadn't.  The hole that she felt in her chest just would not go away. She found it crushing. It was difficult to breathe.

Ria felt the tears pool in the corner of her eyes, again.

At least, last night, she didn't have one of her nightmares. They were always the same.

She walked in a field full of poppies. As she gently ran her hands over the petals, she would look up, and see Morgan leaning against an oak tree. When she made her way towards him, Morgan would turn, and walk into the woods. She'd go after him, but her hands would get wetter. When she glanced down, she'd notice that the poppies were turning into liquid. Before long, she was swimming in the red liquid. She'd feel pressure as she started to go under, trying to get her breath...

Ria always managed to pull herself awake at this point. But even awake there seemed to be a stone was on her chest, stopping her breathe.

During Morgan's absence, Ria experienced a whole spectrum of emotions. Denial, anger, depression, numbness, guilt, and shame.

The guilt and shame were the emotions Ria struggled with the most. The ones that ate at her.

Ria knew in her heart that she loved him, but was devastated that he had gone out of her life without even a goodbye.

Much to her despair, his disappearance had also made her guilty about the night she had spent with him. Ria had *thought* she would be able to give him all of her, to be able to deal with the consequences, but she found she was wrong. It *did* matter very much that she felt as though she had been used. She despised feeling the shame that came with that knowledge.

During her angry moods, she hated him, and was annoyed at herself for falling for, what seemed like now, lies.

*What a fool she'd been to trust him!*

If this was love, Ria was adamant that she would ever love again. She couldn't give herself to anyone one again, only for them to callously trample on her heart.

In her quieter moods, she hated the fact that she still loved him so much. It felt like a physical pain.

Her only consolation was that no one knew about her night with Morgan. She hadn't even had time to share her happiness with her friends before it crashed down around her.

Her family and friends had eventually stopped asking her what was wrong. As much as possible, Ria stayed away from Karen and Sally. Even her parents had stopped questioning her. They'd been concerned and tried to pry out what was wrong, asking where Morgan was. But, after she explained that he had left without saying goodbye, her father stopped asking, and it became more real after voicing it.

Ria tried hard to get back to normal - on the outside at least. She wanted everyone to stop worrying about her. In fact, this evening, Ria had even decided to go out with John. Although, she had stressed to him, as friends.  Tom had arranged it. He seemed desperate to cheer her up. Ria smiled, John always made her laugh, and even though it was the last thing she wanted to do, she agreed.

Ria heard the knock on the door. She forced a smile. Walking over, Ria pulled open the door.

"Hello, beautiful." John stood there, as smiley and as solid as she remembered him.

Ria wasn't silly. She knew the months of crying and eating little had taken its toll on her. She was aware of how drained she looked, but Ria smiled at him for at least trying to make her feel better.

Ria stepped forward to hug him. She found it difficult to let go.

"What a lovely welcome. I would have come before if I knew I would have this reception" John wrapped his arms tightly around Ria, squeezing her. It made him crazy to see her so upset. He *so* wanted to get face-to-face with that loser who had hurt her so badly.

John still loved Ria, and always would, but he'd finally accepted that she didn't feel the same about him. After loving her for so long, it was a very bitter pill to swallow. But, rather than lose her altogether, he was prepared to be a friend. A friend who would help her out of this period in her life. "Come on, let's go and have some fun."

## Chapter 14

Morgan was angry. More angry and frustrated than he could ever remember.

The two months of his father's recovery had taken an enormous toll on him, mentally as well as physically.

The lack of time to eat, the worry, the stress of being heavily relied on, all had Morgan at an all-time low.

Morgan had thought his brother, Darren, would take some of the brunt, so he could rest and recharge. And, more importantly, let him get to Swansea to see Ria. But his mother, in real 'woe-me' style, claimed Darren was too young to *shoulder such responsibilities.*

Morgan had to bite his tongue and rein his temper with his mother.

*Darren was certainly not too young!*

But, when Morgan saw the distress and anguish on her face, he always caved in, and put his mother's grief over his.

Family duty kept him firmly placed.

Morgan was desperate to see Ria, to be in her company. He wanted to be in Swansea, not here.

Even being at home in the evening was now becoming awkward. He'd witnessed yearning flicker on Mary's face too often. So, now, during the day, he wore himself out organising things in the hospital for his parents and problems in the London factory, and during the evenings, he spent walking aimlessly around London.

Initially, Morgan hoped that exercise would help him fall quickly asleep when he eventually flopped into bed.

Unfortunately, that was rarely the case.

Ria haunted his dreams, as well as his waking hours. He so desperately wanted to see her and have him by his side. The need for her was like a crushing physical pain.

Morgan pushed his fingers angrily through his hair. But, to top all of his stresses, every week at the same time, he'd phoned Ria's neighbour, desperate to speak to Ria.

But... he always talked to Tom, never Ria!

Tom *always* had an excuse to why she was not there to talk to him - *Out with friends, gone to the cinema, taking a bath,* even!

Initially, Morgan had taken comfort that she was enjoying herself while he was not there. He *had* thought that she was comfortable with the fact that he was with his father. He *had* thought Tom had passed on the message that he aimed to return soon. It was what had kept him going during this wretched time.

Morgan took a huge breath to calm himself down, his chest constricting painfully in anguish. His love and trust of Ria hadn't made him worry about any of his calls.

Except the last one!

He felt his breath hitch again, trying to restrict his breathing.  He forced himself to breath steadily.

Tom had *calmly* informed him that Ria had gone out for the evening with *John!*  He felt the sick feeling rise again.

*Why would she go out with John when she knew how he felt about her?*

He loved her and wanted to marry her, for goodness sake. Morgan tried hard to kerb his jealousy. He wanted to trust her - but he was human!

He had an uneasy feeling that Ria had gone out with John before him. He was sure *he* was the one he punched at the Christmas party!

He sighed slowly, suddenly feeling very depressed and helpless.  Perhaps, with him being away for so long, her feelings had changed? Perhaps Ria realised that it was John whom she had feelings for? Even though he didn't want to think about that possibility, he knew he had to.

Morgan sat down heavily on the uncomfortable hospital chair. His head in his hands.

*How would he feel if it was John that she wished to be with?*

Jealousy tore through him. Especially at the thought of another man's hands on her.

Morgan rubbed his hands over his face. No, he couldn't let her go back to him without a fight. He loved her too much.

When he lifted his head, he glanced up and down the stark corridor. He'd taken enough. With his decision made, he stood tall. He finally knew he needed to sort this out. Before *he* was the one that ended up in the hospital.


Tom stepped carefully into Ria's bedroom. He was like a man frightened of waking a hibernating bear. Normally, he'd just walk straight in, but he felt too uncomfortable. With himself and with Ria's mood.

Tom gulped, but there was little moisture in his mouth.  When he looked at Ria, he realised he'd let things get totally out of hand. She didn't look at him. Heat claimed his face. He felt guilty. He should've told her about Morgan's phone calls.

Typically, he was laid back about life. But this had changed that. What caused him the most distress was that he had *genuinely* thought, over the months, Ria would have gotten over Morgan Templeton.  She hadn't!

He sighed heavily, worried that Ria hadn't even notice him enter as she stared at the mirror.

Tom had pinned his last hopes on her enjoying her evening with John. He'd trusted the evening would help her get over Morgan.

*Now, he knew he'd been entirely wrong.*

He wasn't protecting her anymore - he was hurting her, and he loved her too much not to admit his guilt.

Tom made a noise, in an attempt to rouse her from her trance. While he waited, Tom felt hot under the collar again. Whichever way it was sugar coated, he wasn't looking forward to admitting that he shouldn't have interfered.

Ria glanced at him in the reflection in the mirror. No smile reached her lips. "Yes, Tom?"

*Here goes! No more justifying his deceit, by the fact that he had never technically lied to anyone!*

As Tom plucked up his courage, his stomach clenched when he remembered Morgan's reaction about John.

*Who could blame him?*

When he'd replaced the receiver, Tom realised that he would feel the same. It was then when he realised he'd been in the wrong.

"What do you want, Tom?" Ria swivelled around.

"Um." Tom looked at her pale face and the purple smudges under her usually sparkling eyes. Guilt ate at him. He'd put her through this. "Ria, I have something to tell you. I don't know where to begin."

Ria's brow furrowed.

Tom continued. "But believe me…I am so sorry if I have hurt you at all."

Ria's eyebrows rose. "What?" she said slowly. The atmosphere had become strange, and the immediate sense of dread put her on edge.

"A couple of months ago, I saw you in a car with that Templeton man…" Tom looked at her, as her eyebrows rose in question.  "But, you had told Mam that you were going to stay the night at Karen's." He straightened his shoulders slightly. He did not like the thought of anyone lying to their mother and, rightly or wrongly, it made him feel that she was not entirely innocent in all of this mess.

The feeling of unease crept up her spine. "Yes."

"After you had spent the night with him, not Karen, like you told us, you started to shut yourself in your room, and cry all the time… Well, he must have done something awful to you."

"What have you done, Tom?" Ria cautiously asked.  She waited for him to look at her again, as his head was lowered.

"Me? Nothing that I punch on the nose wouldn't have solved if he were in Swansea!"

"How do you know he isn't in Swansea, Tom?"  The unease that Ria had been feeling started to spread.

"Like I said, nothing." The rest of the sentence rushed out. "He phoned Doris's house. But I didn't tell you as I thought that he had hurt you!"

"What?" Ria felt her sickness turn into anger. "*When* did he phone?"

"A lot…." He looked at the floor.

Ria stared at her brother's face. Because she knew him so well, she understood his obvious remorse. Some of her anger fled.

*She would forgive him… but not just yet!*

Ria felt too angry and upset to deal with forgiveness yet. "Do you realise what you have done by not telling me?" She struggled to get her words out with the building anger. "I *did* spend the night with him, and then I thought he had forgotten me! I have spent *months* feeling cheapened, regretting the time I spent with him." She waved her arms in frustration. Unshed tears blurred her sight. "I've been so confused, Tom. I felt like a huge part of me had been ripped away, and I had no way of getting it back. And now you tell me that all the while, Morgan had been trying to get hold of me?"

In the silence that followed, Ria suddenly felt hollow. "How could you, Tom? What have you gained from not telling me?" she whispered.

"Nothing, nothing at all. I thought I was helping you. I thought that you would get over him," he argued his case.

"But I *love* him, Tom. How did you think that I could *get over* him?" Tears streamed down her cheeks.

Tom took a tentative step towards her. "I'm so sorry. You'll never know how sorry I am. I *honestly* thought that I was protecting you. I love you and wouldn't ever deliberately hurt you."

Ria stared at him, trying to understand.

A loud sound from downstairs broke the silence. They both turned towards the frantic banging on the front door.

Ria could hear their mother's voice, and then the raised voice of their father.

Ria and Tom looked at each other, puzzled. They kept silent and tried to make out what was going on. It certainly wasn't the usual sounds of the house.

Within minutes, they heard heavy footsteps run up the stairs and along the hallway. Their father shouted.

Ria's bedroom door burst the rest of the way open.

Morgan stood there, as large as life, with a panicked look on his face. His tired eyes eagerly sought out Ria. A ghost of a smile formed on his lips, as he heaved a sigh of relief.

Ria sat motionless.

Morgan strode over to her, unaware of Tom, who stood to the side. Morgan fell to his knees in front of her. It cut him to his bone when he saw her flinch at his actions, and the hurt, confused look in her eyes.

"I've been trying to get hold of you for a month. My father has been ill in hospital. I couldn't get back." Morgan fought back the urge to cry. He grabbed her hands instead. "I've missed you, Ria. I've missed you so much… Ria?"

As his words tumbled out at high speed, Ria just stared at him. She was dumbstruck. Still in shock from Tom's confession, and that fact that Morgan was here in front of her. She wanted to jump up and down, hug him, tell him she loved him - but her body wouldn't respond.

Letting go of her hands, Morgan slowly stood back up. He bent and placed his hands on her face. "Darling, I love you. I don't want you to get back with John. It would break my heart…" Morgan dropped his hands away but continued to look deep into her eyes. "…but if it's really what you want, I won't stop you." He paused, but Ria said nothing. "I will just move back to London, as I couldn't bear to see you with him."

Still numb and trying to work out what was going on, Ria shook her head slowly. "I don't want to be with John…"

Some of the foul tension released in his gut. Seeing an opening, Morgan continued. "I *never* would have left you if I had any control over what happened to my father. I tried desperately to get hold of you. Didn't your brother tell you?"

"No, no I didn't," explained Tom, as he took a step forward.

Morgan swung his head around to the right, previously unaware of Tom, or her parents who stood in the doorway. His concentration had solely been on Ria. Morgan noticed Megan's arm gently restraining Evan.

Morgan tuned back and put his hand on Ria's shoulder. He didn't want to break contact with her.

"I've just told Ria about your calls. I am sorry, I thought I was helping." Tom turned his sad face towards his parents. "And, just for you to know it all, it was me that arranged for Ria to go out with John. I thought she needed cheering up, but I know it was the wrong thing to do."

A surge of anger coursed through Morgan.

*How could Tom be so stupid?*

Morgan clenched his fists, as he battled an urge to knock her brother out. He dismissed the feeling, his primary concern was trying to sort things out with Ria.

Morgan knelt back down and looked directly into her glassy eyes. "I love you Ria, so much. I cannot live my life without you." He used his finger to gently raise her face towards his. "How could you *ever* doubt that? I asked you to marry me, and I even asked your parents' permission before I asked you."

Ria moved her tear-stained eyes towards her parents. "You never told me he asked you," she whispered. She felt Morgan's hand move down to hold her hand.

Megan patted Evan's arm before stepping further into the room. "We were waiting for you to tell us he had asked you to marry him." She glanced at Morgan. "You never did. You ended up crying all the time and saying that he had left. So, we thought that you had had an argument, and that Morgan hadn't asked you." Megan looked back at Evan, before turning to look at Ria once again. "Sorry, darling. We thought we would make it worse telling you that he was going to propose..." She shrugged her shoulders in sadness. "We've all done a fine mess of making you unhappy. Sorry."

While they'd waited patiently by the door, Megan had clearly seen the love pour out of Morgan's. Even though she still could see the wariness in Ria's eyes, Megan could see an intense love burn there too.

Satisfied they would sort it out, Megan turned to her husband, and Tom. "Come on. Let's give them some space to sort this mess out." As she made her way out, she turned briefly. "There's a cup of tea for you both downstairs, for later." She nudged Evan out of the room and sighed. They *all* had some explaining to do to one another.

Ria heard the door click shut and turned back towards Morgan. Her heart constricted when she saw the desperation and, was it, fear in them?

"It looks like we've all done a good job of hurting you, Ria." Morgan walked over to her bed and tapped the space next to him for her to follow. He wanted her to join him, a sign that she still wanted him.

When Ria walked over, his spirits rose. There was hope.

Once she was seated, Morgan turned towards her. "Please, tell me how you are feeling, Ria.   have spent months thinking everything was alright, that you knew that I had to be with my father..." His voice hitched. "Then I thought you had gone back to John, and didn't want me anymore." He grabbed her hands that were held tight in her lap. "I thought that you'd got tired of waiting. Ria, it was like my heart had been torn out. I've never felt anything like it."

Ria took a steadying breath and looked out of the window. He'd opened himself up for her; now it was her turn. She started quietly. "Morgan, I've never been so hurt in my whole life. Especially when you left."

He cringed, understanding her distress.

"They said in work that you were going to *stay* in London... I thought..." she paused, trying to get a grip on her hurt. "...I thought that you had left deliberately, once you had slept with me."

"No."

Ria placed her fingers on his lips to stop his protests. She needed to finish. "I should have trusted my heart, but the gossips made me doubt you. I'm sorry, too." Tears streamed down her cheeks and fell on her cold hands.

Morgan turned her face so she had to looks straight at him. He did not want any more miscommunicating. "Don't be sorry. You haven't done *anything* to harm anyone." He gave her an encouraging smile. "And, I can understand how those malicious gossips might have convinced you that there are love-them-and-leave-them types around. But, I would *never* do that to you. I love you. I have not, and will not, do anything to hurt you intentionally." He tenderly kissed her forehead. "No more mess ups and misunderstandings. You are, and *always* will be, the only one for me."

Morgan reached into his pocket and pulled out the familiar blue box. "Remember this?" He looked straight at her when he opened it.

When she smiled, he took out the engagement ring and slipped it onto her finger.

A perfect fit.

"I had it made smaller for you while I was in London. I thought about you all the time I was there. It was driving me crazy! I would love for you to put the ring on and never take it off. And as soon as can be arranged, I would like it to be joined with a wedding ring..."

"Morgan," Ria whispered.

Morgan gently kissed the end of her tear-stained, wet nose. "Ria you *must* realise how much I love you. I want it all with you - marriage, kids, the works."

Ria hiccupped and stifled back a sob. She tenderly touched his face. "Yes, yes, yes!" she cried, as tears streamed down her face.

But, the tears were not of unhappiness. They were tears of complete and utter joy.

\*\*\*\*

*Thank you for reading this book.  I hope you enjoyed it.*

*As a new author, I would appreciate a review on Amazon. It is the only way that my book gets 'seen'.*

*If you have comments, you can contact me at:* ceribladen@gmail.com

*If you enjoyed this book, find out what happens to Ria's brother, Tom Dillwyn, in 'Copper to Red':* http://www.amazon.co.uk/dp/1482722194

Tom felt Jane stiffen and pull away from his embrace. With a mixture of alcohol, tiredness and contentment, he opened his eyes slowly.  Relaxed.

He wasn't prepared for what he saw.  His eyes began at a sexy pair of low slung heels, travelled up never-ending, shapely legs, moved over the tiniest skirt, up a tight fitting t-shirt, and ended up looking into a pair of smouldering eyes, the colour of malt whiskey.

Tom could have sworn his tongue was on the floor when he croaked out, "Willow?"

Jane was long forgotten.

He thought he caught a look of annoyance flick through Willow's eyes, as she took in the scene.

"Sorry, I didn't realise the snug had turned into a brothel."  Willow could have bitten her tongue off for speaking to customers like that, but she was mad as hell.

"What?" spluttered Jane, as she managed to get the top button of her shift dress done up. Jane hit Tom, wanting him to say something in her defence, annoyed that he was silent.

"What?" The jar to his ribs had made some of the fog clouding his brain clear. "Sorry," he smiled weakly, looking at Willow.

Jane huffed. "That's not what I meant! She insulted me, and you are just sitting there letting her!"

Tom turned his glazed green eyes away from Willow and looked towards Jane. "Well, your dress was undone."

Jane slid him a chilling look. A smack with her handbag made him realise that perhaps his reply wasn't the smartest move his alcohol addled brain could have come up with. He watched her pick up her umbrella and storm out of the snug, shoving Willow as she passed. She threw over her shoulder. "We're finished Tom Dillwyn. Forever!"

He shrugged his shoulders at Willow, who slammed the snug door shut, after scowling at him for a while.

Tom sighed, what was it with the women tonight? He needed to get home, he must have drunk too much...

*ISCA (Roman Fortress) by Ceri Bladen:* Find out what happens between Marcus, a Roman Legionary soldier, and Branwen, a woman from the Silures tribe: http://www.amazon.co.uk/dp/B00CQGB1FY

## *Prologue*
*Isca – 155AD  Night time.  Inside a Silure's roundhouse.*

*Branwen saw a figure walk towards her, through the spring flowers.  She felt her heart flutter; it was Marcus. She knew it was him, for she would recognise him anywhere.*

*He hadn't noticed her yet, hidden amongst the shadows of the trees.  Ignoring the beauty of spring around her; Branwen's attention focused solely on the dark, handsome man walking towards her.  Her man.  Her love.*

*When he was close enough, she stepped out of the shadows into the sunshine. She knew when he had noticed her, as an intimate smile broke over his lips; his teeth white against his olive skin.*

*Their eyes met, locked, and never broke contact as he moved towards her.*

*Staying still, her heart fluttered in her chest as her stomach reeled.  She held her breath as he came closer.*

*It felt like an eternity until she was wrapped in his strong arms. She stayed wrapped in them for a while, safe*

30598834R00123

Printed in Great Britain
by Amazon